REALITY LEAK

JONI SENSEL

REALITY LEAK

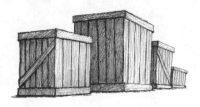

WITH ILLUSTRATIONS BY
Christian Slade

HENRY HOLT AND COMPANY
NEW YORK

For Morgan
—*J. S.*

For Ann
—*C. S.*

Henry Holt and Company, LLC, *Publishers since 1866*
175 Fifth Avenue, New York, New York 10010
www.henryholtchildrensbooks.com

Henry Holt® is a registered trademark of Henry Holt and Company, LLC.
Text copyright © 2007 by Joni Sensel
Illustrations copyright © 2007 by Christian Slade
All rights reserved. Distributed in Canada by H. B. Fenn and Company Ltd.

Library of Congress Cataloging-in-Publication Data
Sensel, Joni.
Reality leak / Joni Sensel ; [illustrated by] Christian Slade.—1st ed.
p.   cm.
Summary: Train noises without trains and mysterious explosions baffle the residents
of South Wiggot as eleven-year-old Bryan and his friend Spot try to connect the strange
happenings with the town's newest industry and its president, Mr. Keen.
ISBN-13: 978-0-8050-8125-1 / ISBN-10: 0-8050-8125-9
[1. Factories—Fiction. 2. Humorous stories. 3. Mystery and detective stories.]
I. Slade, Christian, ill. II. Title.
PZ7.S4784Se 2007   [Fic]—dc22   2006011140

First Edition—2007
Printed in the United States of America on acid-free paper. ∞

10 9 8 7 6 5 4 3 2 1

Imagination embraces the entire world.

—ALBERT EINSTEIN

1

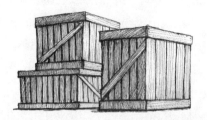

SPECIAL DELIVERY

People did not usually travel down Route 64 stuffed inside wooden crates. Yet here was a crate, a big one, squatting atop the road's dotted line, and somebody odd was about to climb out.

From his LemonMoo stand by the highway, eleven-year-old Bryan Zilcher gaped. Just a minute before, he'd been gazing sadly as a big white semi sped past. He'd been hoping the brake lights might blink. The driver could still turn back to buy a cool drink. He didn't. As the truck bounced over a pothole, the trailer's left rear door had flung itself wide.

A large wooden crate slid from the shadows and tumbled out to the road.

Bryan had braced for an explosion of splinters. Instead of busting on the blacktop, the crate flipped twice, then clunked flat in the center of the road. The truck never slowed. It roared toward the horizon and was gobbled by shimmering heat waves.

Bryan looked both ways down the highway. It stretched along empty, as usual. He eased out to the wooden box, as big as an oven, for a closer look. Nothing hinted at what was inside, but one end of the crate bore a bright orange sticker that said WARNING: DO NOT LICK.

"Why would you want to?" Bryan wondered aloud. Licking a crate seemed a sure way to get slivers in your tongue.

The crate, of course, had not answered. Bryan decided the warning must be in truck-driver slang. Maybe licking was something you did with a forklift. Beneath the orange sticker was a name: Acme Inc. Keeping his tongue safely behind his teeth, Bryan ran his fingers along one wood slat.

The crate might have been waiting for that. Bryan heard the *snick* of some invisible latch. Without even a creak, the lid swung open wide.

Bryan had nearly jumped out of his sandals. Now, from a few yards away, he watched first an arm and then a long, spindly leg crook over the crate's open edge. Slick as scissors, a man clambered out. His white suit and shoes made Bryan think of a preacher or perhaps Colonel Sanders, the fried chicken king. The shiny, gold object he had in his hand was no drumstick, though. It could have been a small flashlight, except one end tapered to a sharp, curly point like the tail of a mechanical pig. The device reminded

Bryan of something unpleasant a dentist might use. He shivered despite the July heat.

The tall man looked directly at him. For an instant, Bryan could have sworn that tiny green spirals twirled in the man's eyeballs. Then those eyes blinked and the spirals vanished. The stranger's eyes were simply an odd green. They made Bryan think of bitter olives without the red pimento stuffed in.

Bryan shook his head. He had to stop spooking himself. It was only some weird-looking guy who'd shown up by accident. It had to hurt to be dumped out of a truck like that, too.

"Are you okay?" he asked.

When the man grinned, Bryan wished he would go back to staring. That grin had too many teeth. It made the stranger look a bit like a jack-o'-lantern.

"Greetings," said Mr. O'Lantern, or whoever he was.

Bryan licked his lips. He considered fleeing to the gas station behind him, but he did not want this man to guess that he was even a bit scared, so he grabbed a paper cup and asked, "Um . . . would you like to buy a glass of my delicious LemonMoo?"

The man twisted his neck slowly to the right, then the left. He pointed his metal device here and there across the farmland and tumbleweeds of South

Wiggot. Used to being ignored, Bryan juggled the cup and wondered if the strange tool took spy photos or measured radiation. He nearly dropped the cup when the creepy visitor finally turned back and replied with a question of his own.

"At what price, may I ask?" The man's voice sounded like he might have a metal gear in his skinny throat instead of an Adam's apple.

Bryan gulped. He usually charged a dollar a cup. But a man in such a well-ironed suit might pay a bit more. He took a deep breath and said, "Two dollars, with ice." He hoped the stranger didn't notice how nervous he felt.

The man tucked his pointy tool into his spotless jacket. When his hand slid back out, he held a small black pouch.

"Of course. Acme Inc. is happy to support local business."

Surprised and excited, Bryan hurried back behind his card table. He felt safer there. He grabbed his LemonMoo pitcher from his dad's ice chest, filled a cup, and dropped in two cubes of ice.

"Archibald Keen, at your service," said the man, waiting. "President of Acme Inc." He unfolded his long fingers and reached to shake hands. Bryan, reminded of a praying mantis, put the cup there instead.

"Uh, hi. My name's Bryan." Hoping to sound as smooth as the stranger, he added, "President of LemonMoo Enterprises."

Mr. Keen looked into the cup, his sharp nose nearly dipping into the yellow milk. For a moment Bryan feared he might suck the drink through his nose. Then he realized Mr. Keen was merely looking at it closely.

"It's like chocolate or strawberry milk. Just lemon instead," Bryan explained.

"Lemon milk?"

"Lemon*Moo*. My own recipe," Bryan added.

"Clever," said Mr. Keen. He took a sip. "Mmm." Or he might have said "Hmm." But he handed Bryan two crumpled bills from his pouch.

Bryan unfolded the bills before he realized what they were—play money from some game. "This is fake," he said.

"Nonsense," said the man, drinking the rest of his LemonMoo in one gulp. "But would you rather have this?" He handed the cup back to Bryan. At the bottom, in a few drops of lemony milk, rested two large gold coins where the ice cubes had been.

Bryan tipped the heavy coins into his hand. Could they be real? He cut off his excitement with a snort. The stranger was just trying to cheat him.

"There's no such thing as gold doubloons," Bryan said. "Or pieces of eight."

"Wrong again," said Mr. Keen. "These, however, are pieces of seven. More lucky than eight. But if you insist—" He reached back into his pouch and pulled out two ordinary dollars. "Perhaps you're not as clever as I thought," he added, handing over the cash.

Ignoring the insult, Bryan took the bills. He offered the coins back to Mr. Keen.

"Keep them," the man said, waving his hand. "Check them out if you like." He looked at his watch. "I must be off. Which way to City Hall, may I ask?"

A laugh and a groan both tried to escape Bryan at the same time. The noise that came out made him sound like a goat. His cheeks hot, he pointed to the gas station, which was stuck with the embarrassing name of Zilcher's Zoom-Juice.

"Right over there. In the office. The mayor's my dad." He quickly bent to replace the pitcher in the ice chest so he wouldn't see Mr. Keen laugh about a gas-pumping mayor. When he peeked up, the stranger was gone.

That wasn't so odd, Bryan decided. With such long legs, Mr. Keen could probably walk pretty fast.

What was strange was the middle of Route 64. The crate was gone, too.

2

A TORNADO OF TRUCKS

By the time Bryan folded up his LemonMoo stand and dragged the ice chest to the gas station office, neither his father nor Mr. Keen could be found. Wrenches and car parts lay strewn all over the floor. On the desk, behind the little sign that read MAYOR, the pages of an auto-parts catalog flipped in the breeze. His father's wiener dog, Oscar, curled in the hubcap that cradled his blanket.

Oscar ran to say hello, and Bryan bent to rub the dog's smooth cinnamon hair.

"Where'd they go, boy?" What might the president of Acme Inc. want with his dad? Maybe Mr. Keen ran a shipping business and traveled around in a crate to advertise his services. It was easier, though, for Bryan to imagine the peculiar man selling voodoo dolls or shrunken heads.

He considered making a quick addition to his secret file of suspicious people and events. Instead he hurried back outside, Oscar trotting behind. If the grown-ups had started down Main Street, Bryan might still catch them.

The Zoom-Juice station squatted at the end of town nearest the highway. Elmer's Eats marked the far end. Bryan could almost have flung a cow pie from one to the other. Between were scattered houses, the feed store, the old farmers' rest home, the Church of Our Lady of the Pea Vines, and the post office, where his dad's girlfriend worked.

The street appeared empty. Mayor Rich Zilcher was too big to miss, especially in his greasy green coveralls. Disappointed, Bryan headed to the post office. Maybe Tripper had noticed the two men going by.

He caught her hanging a new FBI Wanted poster. As he watched through the window a moment, Bryan had to admit he liked Tripper. She told jokes and performed handstands, and her long brown hair was always getting dunked in paint buckets or dish suds or dinner. She looked smart and official in her postal uniform, but the rest of the time she looked like she'd escaped from the circus; her bright clothes never matched. She made the best flapjacks in the county, though, and she would make them any time, day or night. That was enough for Bryan.

She jumped when the bell on the door jingled.

"Oh, it's just you," she said. "Hi."

"Just me?" he huffed. "Hmph! If I was the fugitive on your poster, you'd be in trouble."

"If you were, it wouldn't be too smart to hang around the post office, would it?"

"No, but it would be cool to see your own face on a poster," Bryan said. He imagined "The LemonMoo Legend—Dead or Alive!" splashed across a fuzzy version of his last school photo. His hair was so blond that the skin underneath sometimes tinted it pink, but that wouldn't show on a black-and-white mug shot. Neither would knobby knees or big feet or the strange place where he and Dad lived.

"It wouldn't be cool once they locked you up," Tripper replied. "I'd turn you in so I could be on TV."

"No way," Bryan argued, changing his mind. "If *Crookbusters* ever comes to South Wiggot, they're talking to me." He and his dad never missed the show on TV. It told about ordinary people who had spotted fugitives and helped solve big crimes, and Bryan couldn't wait for his turn to be Crookbuster of the Week. It was one of the things that kept him going during the summer, when he couldn't often see his school friends. Instead he stood at his stand by the highway, peering into every car for a fugitive. His skin tingled at the mere thought of recognizing a crook.

"Okay, you win," Tripper said, picking up a stack of mail. "But I doubt any criminals will ever show up here."

"Some weird guy just did," Bryan said. He shuffled the FBI posters, checking for Mr. Keen's pointy features. It would be hard to mistake a mug like that one. "He wanted my dad. You haven't seen him lately, have you? With a tall, skinny man in a suit?"

Tripper shook her head. "Probably some government inspector. Coming to see if you were bugging me often enough." With a wink, she began flipping envelopes into the old-fashioned wooden slots on the wall.

When none of the sinister faces on the Wanted posters looked familiar, Bryan shoved them away.

Tripper was right. Nothing important ever happened in South Wiggot, and nobody important lived there— including him. He heard it often enough at school, didn't he? The few kids who lived in South Wiggot rode a bus to the next town for classes, and the other students never let them forget they were misfits and hicks. Bryan, for his part, was known mostly as Zilcher the Zero.

He sighed and hoisted himself onto the counter to watch Tripper sort mail. If he'd been more than a zero, one of those slots would hold fan letters and interview requests, or at least a card from his mother once in a while. Instead he only got to collect the gas station's bills.

Tripper glanced at him. "Sell all your LemonMoo already?"

"Fat chance." Bryan rolled his eyes. He'd never sold more than a few cups a day, and Tripper bought most of those. The LemonMoo Legend was a joke. If he got tired of being Zilcher the Zero, he could always be the LemonMoo Loser instead.

He blew wisps of hair off his forehead, trying to banish his grouchy thoughts. "I did sell a little, though," he said, "to the guy in the—"

The bell on the door made a racket. Bryan's dad

stood there, jiggling the door. A two-foot wrench teetered half out of his coveralls pocket.

"Ta da!" said Bryan's dad. "Can I get a round of applause, please?" Oscar, who'd been left on the sidewalk, ran in to spin excited circles around Dad's boots.

Bryan hopped off the counter to peer out the window for Mr. Keen. The sidewalk was empty. Way down the street, three old coots gazed up at the sky, probably discussing the weather. If the newcomer was still out there, he must have hidden in somebody's Dumpster.

"What are we celebrating?" asked Tripper.

"Guess what your loyal mayor just signed?"

"A law," Bryan guessed, "making *me* the town sheriff!" He slipped a drawl into his voice as he added, "Ya got two hours to get outta South Wiggot, Pa."

"Elsewise, cowpoke," added Tripper, "you'll be buzzard meat by nightfall."

Dad ignored their joking. "Lease papers!" he said, waving them like a winning lottery ticket. "South Wiggot just got a new business!"

"Not Mr. Keen?" Bryan wondered.

"Did you meet him?"

"He bought some LemonMoo," Bryan began. "And I saw him get here in a—"

"He must have liked it, pal!" Dad crowed, clapping Bryan on the back. He sounded so proud it almost made up for his rude interruption. "Or maybe he figured if the town was good enough for your business, it was good enough for his!"

"What kind of business is it?" asked Tripper.

Dad's smile wavered. "I'm not really sure. They're leasing the old TaterNugget plant, plus the five acres behind it."

"I hope they don't get too much mail." Tripper looked around her tiny office. Her eyes fell on the FBI posters. "You're certain it's all legal, though, right?"

Tripper liked to suspect things. Bryan liked to give her things to suspect, so he said quickly, "He seemed kind of creepy to me. His eyeballs twirled, too."

"That doesn't sound like a businessman." Tripper grinned. "That sounds more like Mesmo, Master of Hypnosis. Did he tell you to cluck like a chicken?"

"Actually, he kinda looked like a chicken," Bryan said. "A tall, plucked chicken with teeth."

"I can see this good news is wasted on you two," grumbled Bryan's dad.

"I'm sorry. We're just having fun." Tripper peeked at his papers. "So what's this great company called?"

"Acme Inc."

Over Dad's shoulder Tripper read, "Astro-Chrono-Magical Enterprises—that's what ACME stands for?"

"Magical?" Bryan repeated. Maybe Mr. Keen bottled conjuring oil or printed spell books. Bryan stuffed his hand in his pocket to make certain his gold coins hadn't vanished.

"Weird name," Tripper continued. "What's it mean?"

"It means jobs and new people in town," said Bryan's dad. "Not to mention customers for my station. And for LemonMoo, too!" He beamed at his son.

"I wonder what they're gonna make," Bryan said.

"Pollution, probably," Tripper muttered. "You should have asked a few questions, Rich. What if they make dynamite? Or toxic waste?"

"What if they cut ladies in half?" Bryan teased. "Or make all the rabbits in town disappear?"

"In a TaterNugget factory?" Dad replied. "Don't be sill—"

WHAM! The door slammed open. The same gust of wind sent letters flying.

"Whoa!" Tripper clutched at flying mail. "Is it a tornado?"

Bryan hurried to the window, where the glass rattled in the frame.

A big white truck zoomed past outside. Another followed, then another. Each was perfectly white, blank, and just like the one that had delivered Mr. Keen not long ago.

"What the heck?" After grabbing the door to stop it from slamming again, Bryan's dad stepped into the dust swirling in the street. Bryan hurried behind.

Another truck approached, an Acme logo plain on the cab.

"Guess they're moving in, huh?" Bryan said.

"That was quick!" exclaimed his father.

The trucks rumbled toward the old TaterNugget factory on the hill. The place had been deserted for years. Apparently not enough people wanted lumps of squished spuds. A chain-link fence stood around the plant's parking lot, but the gate was wide open now. White trucks poured through like milk.

Tripper peered out the doorway behind them, her arms full of windblown mail.

"What's that?" She pointed.

One last truck roared through the dust. As it passed, dozens of white papers fluttered down.

Bryan ran to grab one. He read the big black letters aloud.

❖ **PUBLIC MEETING** ❖

SPONSORED BY ACME INC.

Church of Our Lady of the Pea Vines

7 P.M. sharp

Come one, come all.

 Free food!

"What could that be about?" Tripper asked.

"Maybe they want to introduce themselves," said Dad.

"Free food," Bryan repeated. It didn't say anything about drinks. If the whole town showed up, he might get a few customers for his LemonMoo stand.

Clenching the flyer in his fingers, he ran off down the street. "I'd better go mix another batch!"

First, though, he had something more important to make.

3

THE PILLOWCASE FILES

Bryan slipped through the gas station office to the garage bay his father had remodeled after the divorce. He would never have told Dad how much teasing their home earned him, but he did love where he slept. The world's tallest bunk bed was now up near the ceiling on the hydraulic lift. Bryan lowered his bed with the remote control, then he climbed aboard and raised it again to make sure he would not be disturbed.

The only boy in the county with a bed on a hydraulic lift also may have been the only one with a file cabinet in his pillow. No wood or metal was involved, so it wasn't as uncomfortable as it sounds. Bryan simply kept his pillow in two pillowcases, rather than one. Arranging the openings at opposite ends kept the contents secret and snug.

Bryan tugged off the first pillowslip and reached into the second to pull out his pillowcase files. He called them files, even though they were really manila envelopes, because he knew that detectives on *Crookbusters* kept case files. His had remained empty a long while, but now he had a file labeled "Unsolved" for last year's feed store robbery and another containing the names of kids at school rumored to heist lunch money ("Junior Crooks"). A third file held notes about local oddballs such as the two high school students who dressed so goth they looked like refugees from Halloween ("Suspects"). Tripper's name was in that file, too; just because Bryan liked her didn't place her above suspicion.

His pillow also concealed an envelope unrelated to crime. "Important Ideas and Inventions" had been scrawled on the outside. So far the only thing inside was his LemonMoo recipe.

Shoving all these aside, Bryan peeked into his newest file, the one labeled "Freaky." It contained only two items: a plastic bubble wand and a clipping from the *Wiggot Weekly*.

The bubble wand had belonged formerly to three-year-old Alison Merk. A few days ago, Bryan had spotted the girl blowing bubbles on her front porch. Instead of the usual globes, the glimmering liquid had formed fat alphabet letters that drifted a few feet, then popped. Bryan had gaped for ten minutes, amazed. He'd seen giant bubbles and wiener-shaped bubbles, and bubbles that could be touched without popping, but never bubbles in the shape of an *F* or a *W*. The girl, who lost interest before he did, had been thrilled to take two dollars in exchange for the wand. Bryan had never managed to repeat her results, though, or even find another witness. Now he was just waiting to see if Alison Merk got sick, sprouted horns, or grew up to be a genius.

The newspaper clipping reported something more mundane, at least for South Wiggot. An ad for last month's county fair included a photo of a Holstein calf with an unusual black spot. The headline read COME SEE THE QUESTIONING CALF! The blotch on the calf's flank did indeed look just like a question mark, complete with the little dot at the bottom. The proud owner had boasted, "I've seen cows with spots shaped like Jesus and the state of Texas, but this is my first punctuation! I'm hoping we'll win a prize."

Having seen a few odd cow spots himself, Bryan

had saved the clipping to remind himself that *Crook-busters* was not the only way to get noticed.

Now he borrowed the pen out of his "Suspects" envelope long enough to jot the date and Mr. Keen's name on the Acme flyer, along with "arrived in a crate" and "gold coins." He folded the paper and stuffed it in with the bubble wand and the newspaper ad. He could grab another envelope the next time he passed through his dad's office and decide later how to label the file for Acme.

Big white trucks zoomed down the road all afternoon. After so much commotion, most of the puny town turned out for the meeting. Old-timers sat in the first four church pews, just like on Sunday. A dozen younger townsfolk clustered outside, muttering and looking uncomfortable.

Bryan set up his LemonMoo stand next to the big double doors. No one from Acme had arrived by 7:10 P.M., so people got restless and thirsty. As he poured, Bryan overheard a few odd conversations. The lady who ran the rest home passed around a baseball she swore she'd found inside an orange peel instead of the fruit. An old geezer with no teeth (but a known fondness for pranks) gazed into the sky and mumbled about black-and-white rainbows. Later, one of the few boys near Bryan's age told anyone who would listen that on Saturday his pet snake had laid a golden egg. Of course, the snake owner had a reputation for sniffing fertilizer and telling whoppers. In fact, that combination had undoubtedly caused a good deal of the prejudice against South Wiggot at school.

Customers kept Bryan too busy filling cups to ask questions, but the snake story reminded him of his gold coins. While making change for Pastor Daniels, he pulled them from his pocket. The pastor was one of the smartest and, presumably, most honest people in town.

"Do these look like real gold to you?" Bryan asked.

Pastor Daniels bounced one of the coins in his age-spotted hand. For an instant Bryan feared he might bite into the gold the way pirates did on TV. He didn't want to get blamed for breaking the pastor's old teeth! Instead, the pastor scraped at the coin with a key.

"Might be the real thing," he said. He held the coin aloft. The setting sun glinted off the metal. Wishing the pastor wouldn't flash it around so much, Bryan glanced nervously at the crowd.

Nobody noticed the shining thing in the pastor's hand—nobody, that is, except Spot. Bryan groaned.

The goofy girl trotted over, her braids flopping like ears on a puppy. For this girl, "mutt" was no insult. The dog collar on her neck gleamed with metal studs all around. Sometimes she painted her nose black. People called Spot the Dog Girl of South Wiggot. She was a year behind Bryan in school, and normally he saw her only at the bus stop.

"Woof," she said. Bryan scowled. It was true that everyone knew her, but who wanted to be famous for being a weirdo?

"Hi, Spot," he mumbled, stirring his LemonMoo to avoid looking at her.

His eyes still on the coin, Pastor Daniels said, "Hello, Rebecca," to Bryan's surprise. Almost nobody used Spot's real name.

She eyed the gold coin briefly, then her gaze shifted to Bryan's pitcher. She held her hands like paws under her chin, her tongue lolling, begging.

"One dollar," Bryan grumbled. Looking more like a human being, Spot dug a crumpled bill out of her pocket. He took her money and handed her a cup. She wiggled her backside, as if she had a tail to wag, then lapped at her drink with her tongue. Bryan couldn't watch. Even if *she* wasn't embarrassed, he was.

Luckily, Pastor Daniels was talking. "If this coin

is real, it's probably worth a bushel," he said. "Where did you get it?" As he started to hand Bryan's coin back, it flew out of his fingers, a tiny shooting star arcing into the crowd.

"My coin!" Bryan exclaimed.

"Heavens! I don't know how I did that!" Pastor Daniels swiveled his head, unsure where it had gone.

Spot put down her LemonMoo and darted into the crowd. Short and skinny, she slipped under elbows and between legs before their owners even noticed her there. Bryan had barely come around his table when Spot reappeared.

She trotted up to him, the gold coin trapped neatly between grinning lips. Her eyes glowed. Bryan had seen that look of success many times on Oscar's doggy face. He only hoped she'd picked up the coin with her hand, not her teeth. The idea of Spot's nose in the dust made him cringe.

"What a quick girl," said the pastor. "You saved my mistake."

Bryan held out his hand. The coin dropped neatly into his palm, mercifully dry and spit-free.

"Good fetch," he told Spot. She had her own page in his pillowcase files, but he had to admit she'd just done him a favor. "You are so weird," he added, "but thanks!"

Smirking, she shyly extended one hand, palm cupped toward the ground. For an instant, Bryan thought she expected him to give her the coin. Then he got it. He gave her the doggy handshake she'd asked for.

Just then a white truck roared up to the church. It stopped with a gasp of the air brakes. Nearly every face in the crowd turned toward the cab to see who would get out.

Only Bryan watched the rear doors of the trailer instead.

4

ACME ARRIVES WITH A BANG

Apparently Mr. Keen did not always travel by crate. The tall fellow unfolded himself out of the truck cab and slammed the door. Bryan's disappointment dissolved when he reminded himself that he alone had witnessed Mr. Keen's first arrival. That small secret pleased him.

The Acme chief held a slide projector under one arm. With the other, he waved everyone inside. His movements jerked at double-speed like windshield wipers in a downpour.

"Chop chop—no time to lose!" shouted Mr. Keen.

"Seven sharp, didn't we say? Countdown! Five, four, three . . ." His long legs carried him quickly into the church. Pastor Daniels hurried after, looking alarmed, as though he expected Mr. Keen to actually blast off or maybe explode.

Watching them go, Spot curled her lip, growling. Bryan gave her a shrug, but he knew what she meant. Mr. Keen made you wonder if you should bite him or run away. When she slunk cautiously through the church doorway, he followed, leaving one door open to keep watch on his LemonMoo stand.

Inside, all eyes were on Mr. Keen, who had stopped near the front. When Pastor Daniels caught up, the Acme boss promptly handed him the slide projector and stepped up onto the first pew.

The pastor, who was used to being in charge, juggled the projector in his arms. "Blessings, all," he began, "and thank you for coming. Please welcome Mr. . . . uh . . ."

Towering above him, Mr. Keen set his hand atop Pastor Daniels's gray head as if the pastor, not Spot, went around acting like a pooch. Bryan could see the funny look on the pastor's face all the way from the back of the church.

"Keen, Archibald Keen," the newcomer

announced. "Pleased to be part of your fine community." Two or three people clapped politely.

"Let me introduce Acme Inc." Mr. Keen tapped the projector in the pastor's arms. Light shot out, spreading a big white rectangle on one wall. Impressed, Bryan wondered how many batteries the

hidden power pack took. The rectangle jiggled when the pastor shuffled his feet.

"Steady, steady . . . very good!" said Mr. Keen. The projector clicked. An Acme logo blazed on the wall, then a photo of the old factory from beyond the front gate. Bryan had tried to climb that gate more than once. He'd never gotten past the barbed wire up top.

Mr. Keen cleared his throat. "Astro-Chrono-Magical Enterprises is an international corporation vending a unique agricultural product to elite organizations, institutions, and exceptional individuals."

Bryan blinked. He'd barely understood a single word, other than *agricultural*—you couldn't live in a farm town without knowing that one. Mr. Keen talked fast, like he was reciting in class and wanted his turn to be over quick.

The slide projector clicked faster, flipping through pictures of something lumpy and brown. It looked like photos of dirt.

It *was* dirt. "We're very excited about the local growing medium," Mr. Keen said. "You must be very proud of your soil."

Heads nodded. Bryan rolled his eyes. Farmers in South Wiggot loved to talk about two things—weather and dirt. Nearby, somebody grumbled, "Aw, them acres behind the factory ain't nothing but rocks and weeds."

The slide show had already moved on. Bits of machinery, glass pipes, wood crates, and big hoses glowed on the wall, every photo more blurry than the one before.

"Multiple patents protect the state-of-the-art blah-de-blah technology we use in Acme's proprietary processing processes."

Bryan wasn't certain he'd heard right, but nobody else seemed disturbed. The townsfolk all squinted at the fuzzy slides. Only Spot, who had sidled up to Bryan, tipped her head quizzically. She whined in her throat. It sounded like "Rrrruuh?"

"Did he just say 'blah-de-blah'?" Bryan whispered.

She nodded uncertainly. "Yip."

Bryan focused again on Mr. Keen's words. ". . . As a token of our goodwill, Acme will offer free dental service to everyone within twenty miles of—"

Ker-bOOOM! A huge explosion echoed outside. The audience gasped. A candle on the altar tipped over.

"What was that?" at least five people asked.

Bryan's dad jumped to his feet. "The gas pumps!"

"No, no, not to worry. Be seated, please." Mr. Keen hopped down to stop him. "A minor side effect, that's all, as we're getting set up. I should have warned you. You may hear the odd noise or two."

Bryan peered out the door. The Zoom-Juice pumps gathered dust down the road. The factory wasn't on fire. Nothing in town looked awake, let alone explosive.

"It won't happen again," Mr. Keen continued. Bryan flashed an "okay" sign at his dad. Mr. Keen had a good hold on Dad's elbow anyway as he added, "It's only—"

Ka-POW!

"—a few tests!" the man from Acme shouted over the crowd's worried murmurs. "Completely routine!"

Pastor Daniels spoke up. "Explosions, for heaven's sake? How often—"

"Never! Not at all! Utterly the last one, I assure you—"

Ka-pffff. The third noise, much softer, sounded like a big bottom sitting down hard on a small vinyl cushion. That seemed to reassure the crowd. It certainly pleased Mr. Keen.

"Good, very good." He showed his jack-o'-lantern smile. "From here on we're as quiet as lard—you'll hardly know Acme's in town. Questions?"

Several hands went up.

"Hey, where's our free food?" someone called.

"My word, I forgot," Mr. Keen said. He reached into his jacket and pulled out a huge chicken drumstick. He looked at it in surprise, then stuffed it back out of sight. When he brought out his long fingers again, they held a wad of money. "All you can eat down the street! Acme supports local business!" He handed the cash to the man who ran the café.

"We'll stay open late!" Elmer declared, counting bills as fast as he could.

"Excellent, thank you, good day," replied Mr. Keen. While the audience chattered about all you can eat, he grabbed his projector and made fast for the door. He aimed straight for Bryan. Although people with questions reached out to slow him, Mr. Keen slipped between them like a wet watermelon seed. For an instant Bryan thought he and Spot would be trampled under those shiny white shoes.

Then Tripper stepped into the path, her arms wide to block it. Mr. Keen's legs scissored to a stop.

"Wait," Tripper said. "What do you grow?"

"What's Chrono-Magical mean, anyway?" Bryan piped up.

"Excellent question, thank you," Mr. Keen told Tripper. "We reap what we sow, of course. So glad you reminded me—" Sidestepping her, he turned back to the crowd.

"Planters and painters needed immediately! Good wages. Excellent dental benefits. Accepting applications tomorrow between eight-fifty-six and nine-oh-seven A.M. Please be prompt!" He pulled a stack of forms from the side of his coat where the chicken leg had vanished and flung them toward the crowd. Papers flapped before they were snatched from midair or left to drift down to the floor.

When the fluttering cleared, the man from Acme was gone.

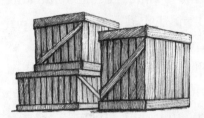

5

QUESTIONS, CODES, AND A QUIZ

"Cloned carrots," suggested Bryan's dad. He and Tripper were helping Bryan haul his Lemon-Moo stand home after the Acme meeting. Dad held the station door open. "Or three-headed cabbages. Growing that would take some fancy technology."

"I'd like chocolate chip potatoes," Bryan said, his arms full of paper cups. "I wish someone would invent that."

Tripper stashed Bryan's card table against the wall. "Okay, sure, there's some weird food out there," she said. "But what kind of farming makes explosions?"

"Danny Soose told me their manure tank exploded

one time," Bryan offered. "It rained cow plop for ten minutes."

Tripper ignored him. "Besides, what can they grow on five acres? That's not enough land for any kind of food crop."

Bryan had his own theories. He thought the word *magic* in their name was a clue. Maybe Acme grew magic jumping beans or green beans that worked like spinach for Popeye. Magic beanstalks might even explain his gold coins! He kept his ideas to himself. The adults rarely listened to him anyway.

"Lots of people in town need jobs," said Bryan's dad. He sank into the chair behind his desk. "Once they get hired, they can fill us in."

He and Tripper kept talking about taxes and pollution and paychecks. No longer listening, Bryan emptied his pockets into the coffee can where he kept his LemonMoo fund. Not enough paper money muffled the jingle. He'd never be able to afford a computer with nothing but quarters and dimes. No computer meant no e-mail, no Internet gaming, no instant messaging—and another summer with no friends.

Bryan slapped the lid back on his can, knocking away the gloom that threatened to overtake him. He could at least pick up the phone and see if Mark or Effanus was at home. First, though, still thinking about his noisy coffee can, he drew an Acme job application from his back pocket. He'd swiped one from under a pew. After pulling up a stool, he found a pencil and wrote his name at the top of the form, just under a spot of fried chicken grease.

Bryan had never filled out a job application, but he'd completed forms for school and for contests in the newspaper. This form was not like any of those. He got through the first few questions all right. He was right-handed and equipped with the usual number of toes. He'd never had a single cavity—Lemon-Moo helped with that. And as far as he knew, he had never been kidnapped by aliens.

He wasn't sure about the next question, though, and he definitely couldn't remember. "Hey, Dad," he said, "was I born under a full moon?"

The adult conversation stopped. "Beats me," Dad replied. "Why?"

"I guess I'd better mark 'unknown.'"

Tripper moved to look over his shoulder. "Hold it." She swiped the pencil out of his hand.

"Hey," Bryan complained.

"Listen to these questions," Tripper said. "'Have you ever seen fairies or elves? Do you have a steel plate in your head?'" She shot a glance at Bryan's dad. "What kind of job application is this?"

"It's *my* kind." Bryan grabbed back his pencil. If she could be rude, so could he.

"You can't work there," she told him.

"Why not? I can plant seeds. Or paint crates or whatever."

"You're not old enough, for starters."

"I am so. There's a space right here: 'fourteen or under.' I'm under." Bryan marked that box.

Tripper scowled. "You might get poisoned or sucked into some machine. Or blown up. There could be more explosions."

Bryan's hands clenched. Usually Tripper's suspicions were funny. Not this time.

"Dad?"

"Well, pal, Tripper might have a good point," Dad said. "Maybe we—"

Jumping off his stool, Bryan shot Tripper the nastiest look he'd ever given a grown-up.

"You're not my mother!" He snatched the application. Before anyone could yell, he ran out.

Bryan had never argued with Tripper before. Nobody but his official parent was going to tell him what to do, though. Had his father said no? Not exactly. And his mother? He hadn't seen her for almost two years. Dad was the only one now. It would probably be smartest, however, if Bryan didn't

37

wait until tomorrow to apply for that job. He walked up the hill toward the factory gate.

Three trucks sat on the far side of the fence. Bryan tried not to think about their dark windows staring ominously as he approached. He walked tall, like a businessman holding a briefcase of money instead of his crumpled job application.

When no guard came out of the gatehouse, Bryan pressed his face against its dusty window. As though his nose had tripped a button, an air horn atop the gatehouse honked briefly and the gate rattled open. He jumped. If he'd really been carrying a briefcase of money, he would have dropped it. Hurrying inside the fence, he eyeballed the gate, afraid it might shut on him like a trap. It yawned, motionless.

Not a single window interrupted the high concrete walls of the building. On one side, a small office jutted out like a square wart. Bryan trotted over and knocked on the door.

He tried to knock, that is. Instead of *knock, knock,* the door went *eek, eek!* under his knuckles. Startled, he ran his hand over the cool metal. It felt ordinary enough. When no one answered, he hit it harder. Instead of a bang or even a double-loud *eek,* the door whined like a ray gun in a movie, then swung wide. There stood Mr. Keen.

"Orange?" asked Mr. Keen.

"Excuse me?" By now Bryan wasn't sure his ears were working right.

"Fifty-seven," replied Mr. Keen.

Certain he'd heard correctly this time, Bryan blinked. Was Mr. Keen crazy? Was it part of a "knock-knock" joke? He decided the man's unusual greeting must be a password. He had no idea what the counter password might be, but it couldn't hurt to guess.

"Um . . . brella?" Bryan expected the door to slam in his face. Instead, Mr. Keen smiled.

"Close enough," he said. "Umbrella to you, too. Please come in."

The small white room was nearly empty. Each wall held a door. One door had been painted blue, one glowed yellow, and one was red. Chairs were stacked in a corner. A very large clock face looked down from the ceiling, its hands twirling like blades on a lopsided fan. Bryan watched the clock spin and wondered how it could possibly tell time.

"What can Acme Inc. do for you?" Mr. Keen stood in the center of the room, his hands clasped. Bryan was glad to hear a regular question. He wouldn't get very far talking in code.

"I'd like to apply for a job." He handed Mr. Keen his application.

The Acme chief barely glanced at the wrinkled page. Looking Bryan over carefully, he asked, "How many eggs in a dozen? You might call this a test."

Relieved to get such an easy question, Bryan replied, "Twelve."

"How many months in a year?"

"Twelve again."

Mr. Keen's eyes narrowed. "Aha. So—how many eggs in a year?"

"Uh . . . boiled or fried?" Bryan asked. He was stalling for time.

"Deviled."

Bryan pondered. Twelve seemed like a good answer, but it might be too obvious. Besides, he ate a lot more than twelve eggs in a whole year. He probably ate that many at Easter alone. Plus deviled eggs were cut in half, so that might double the number—

"You don't know, do you?"

Bryan bit his lip. He felt his new job melting like ice. "Twenty-four?" he blurted out.

"The answer is eggteen, of course. I will give you some credit, however, for guessing. So here is another: Name the square root of the letter *H*."

Bryan looked at his sneakers to think. He was sure there was no such number as eggteen. What's more, he didn't think letters of the alphabet got into math until algebra. His class had already studied square roots, though. He knew that two was the square root of four because two times two equals four. Thinking about four gave him an idea. If you turned it upside down, a **4** looked very much like a small letter **h**. And once you started looking at it that way, a capital **H** had a bunch of **4**s in it. Four fours, in fact.

He took a deep breath and said, "Four?"

Surprise and pleasure lit Mr. Keen's face. "You're hired! Come back tomorrow at nine. Seed stomping will start right away."

Excited, Bryan grinned and wiggled his toes. Then he asked, "How much do you pay?"

"We'll discuss wages tomorrow. See you then." Mr. Keen shook Bryan's hand and swept him to the door. "By the way, did you check out those pieces of seven?"

"Sort of," Bryan answered.

"Lucky, no?"

Still flushed from passing his test, Bryan nodded. "I guess so."

"You owe me a LemonMoo, then!" Mr. Keen said cheerily, shutting the door.

"Deal," Bryan said to himself. He spun on his

heels and broke into a run. He couldn't wait to share the news—he, Bryan Zilcher, had just become the town's first Acme employee!

Even before the gate rattled shut behind him, doubt dragged Bryan back to a walk. What if Dad wouldn't let him go to work in the morning? He might have to keep his new job a secret. Bryan loved secrets, but a secret like this would be trouble to keep—and even more trouble if it got loose.

6

TROUBLE WITH
A CAPITAL T

By the time he got back to the Zoom-Juice station, Bryan's excitement was tangled with guilt in his belly. He slipped into the garage bay, trying to ignore the buzzing of the fluorescent lights. It sounded like scolding. Below them, the TV blared at their sofa—the back seat of an old Buick sedan. No one was watching the show.

"Hey, Dad, are you here?" Bryan called. His voice bounced off the concrete.

Then he spotted the note. On an air-filter box near the TV, Dad had scrawled, "Out looking for Oscar. If he comes home, keep him in. Dad."

Bryan snorted. It sometimes seemed that his father, who lost Oscar at least once a month, worried more about his dog than his son. Unlike a certain runaway mother, Oscar always turned up. Sometimes it just took a few hours.

Bryan snapped his fingers. If anyone knew where to find the pesky pooch, Spot would. And if he brought the dog home himself, maybe his good deed would pay off.

He jogged to Spot's house and was about to knock on the door when he heard a muffled "oof." Bryan peered into the gloom of the yard. Spot lay flat on her back under a shrub. A huge Saint Bernard sat on her belly, sliming her with dog kisses.

"Hey, have you seen Oscar? You know, our dachshund?" Bryan eyed the hairy beast pinning Spot. He hoped it hadn't gobbled Oscar for a snack.

"Ummph," groaned Spot. She didn't bark, growl, or whine. "Get him off."

Bryan's eyebrows shot up. "Hey, you can talk!"

Spot only glared.

With one eye on the dog's wagging tail and the other on its slobbery muzzle, Bryan found the collar half hidden in the Saint Bernard's scruff. He wrapped both hands around it and tugged. The huge animal barely moved, but Spot wiggled out.

She hopped up and drew a deep breath, then wiped her face dry on the dog's fluffy shoulder. Afraid Spot might thank him by licking his cheek, Bryan stayed back.

Instead, she grinned and said, "Ruff. Thanks. He's a stray. I was playing with this." She blew on a small silver tube—a silent dog whistle. The Saint Bernard raced around her feet, then heaved itself onto its hind legs as if asking to dance. This time Spot dodged carefully out of reach.

Bryan noticed a plastic pouch on the dog's collar. "Is there something in that? Like those rescue dogs in the Alps?"

When the dog dropped again to all fours, Spot fumbled for the pouch. She reeled out a thin strip like a cash register receipt, but bearing a note. Bryan read, "'Not much Trouble yet. The locals don't seem to suspect. Will advise. Keen.'"

Bryan's breath came faster. He read it again. "What don't we suspect?"

Spot shrugged. Her pigtails flopped against her cheeks.

"I just got hired by Mr. Keen," Bryan told her. "Do you think he's—hey!" The Saint Bernard ripped the note from their hands and ran off. The white curl of paper trailed from its teeth. By the time

Bryan and Spot had chased it around the corner of the house, the messenger dog had sped out of sight.

"Try that whistle again!" Bryan suggested.

Two German shepherds and the pastor's poodle came sniffing around, but the Saint Bernard didn't return. Oscar didn't show up, either.

Tripper appeared, however, looking windblown and breathless. As she approached, she peered at the dogs crowding Spot's knees.

"There you are. Is Oscar with you?" Tripper asked Bryan.

"No. I was looking for him." He turned away. He didn't feel like talking to her.

"I thought maybe he followed you when you left." Tripper's eyes moved between Bryan and Spot. "Have you been here ever since?"

Bryan groaned. He didn't want Tripper to think the Dog Girl was his girlfriend, but he didn't want to admit he'd been to the factory, either. He may not have noticed Oscar behind him at first. He was sure, though, that he'd been alone by the time he'd knocked on the factory door.

"No, but we'll find him," he muttered. He waved for Spot to come along, then set out into the twilight.

Spot eyed him curiously but followed. Tripper fell in beside them.

"We don't need any help," he told Tripper. The words clunked like rocks between them. Spot puffed into her silent whistle like she wished it could drown out the tension.

"I know," Tripper said. "I just wanted to apologize for butting in about your job application. That should be between you and your dad."

"Oscar!" Bryan scanned the fields. Tripper stuck to him like wet oatmeal.

"And see, out here in the dark, you don't have to look at me or say 'oh, it doesn't matter' or 'apology accepted,'" Tripper said. "I hate saying that before I really mean it. But at least you know I'm sorry." She stopped walking.

Bryan kept going, hunting for dog shapes in the shadows.

"I'll let you two search this way," Tripper added.

"Whatever."

She did sound sorry, but he was still kind of mad. Plus he wanted to think about the Saint Bernard's strange note. After the fight over his job application, there was no way he'd tell Tripper about that.

"I'll go check if he's turned up at the station yet,"

Tripper finished. "See you there." She veered off and her calls for Oscar grew distant. Once she'd passed out of sight, Bryan headed toward Acme. Maybe the dopey dog had gotten trapped inside the gate.

Spot searched one side of the road. He took the other. As they drew near the factory, Bryan wondered what kind of Trouble, with a capital *T*, Mr. Keen had meant. "Not much Trouble yet" sounded as if plenty might still be expected. Maybe Bryan's new boss was a gang leader or mobster. That might explain the passwords. Of course, spies used passwords, too, and caused all kinds of trouble. Something was fishy, for sure. Why else would a grown man send messages with a dog?

When a late Acme truck rattled past them, washing them with warm summer air, Bryan's eyes narrowed. He'd love a peek inside.

Spot watched the truck careen up the hill. "Is he smart about cars?"

"Mr. Keen?"

"Osc—ruh-roh, look!" Spot pointed at a limp blob on the dotted line up ahead.

7

A FLAT FIND

Bryan nearly choked on his heart. The dark blob on the road had four legs, a tail, and a long wiener body. It was colored like Oscar, too. But he'd seen roadkill before, and it had never been like this.

Spot gasped. "Oh no! He—hmm?" She tipped her head. A puzzled whine squeaked from her throat.

Bryan forced himself to bend close. If the shadow in the road was his father's dog, it was the flattest, smoothest, least gooey dead thing he'd ever seen. He poked it. It felt like a cold pancake left on the table all day. Lifting one edge, he peeled it off the blacktop.

"Yuck!" Spot scrambled away.

The back side of the blob was as flat and smooth as the front. "I don't think it's real," Bryan said. "It looks kinda like Oscar, but it's more like—like an Oscar mouse pad. See?" He held it toward her.

A slow growl emerged through Spot's clenched teeth. She inched one finger toward the floppy form. Her growl ended in a high note of surprise. The blob wobbled at her touch.

"It's rubber. Or no, this part's hairy, but . . . it must be a toy." Bryan folded the dog thing and stuffed it into his pocket. Spot watched uneasily.

"Is it a joke?"

"Let's keep looking."

They searched until it was too dark to see. Spot's mouth dropped open as she followed Bryan into the Zoom-Juice station. Seeing the mishmash of furniture and car repair gear through her eyes, Bryan felt his scalp prickle with heat.

Dad slumped on the sofa, staring at Oscar's dog dish. Tripper perched nearby, patting his shoulder. Only she looked up when Bryan came in with Spot.

"You didn't find him?" Tripper asked.

"He's gone for sure this time," Dad sighed.

Spot looked at Bryan's pocket and whined. He wished he could kick her.

"We did find something," he said. Reluctantly, he reached into that pocket. His fingers touched what felt like the tongue of a shoe. Then his hand was shoved back out by scrabbling claws. Oscar, whole and 3-D, leapt into Dad's arms.

"Oskie!" crooned Dad.

"Aaaaoooo!" Spot howled in surprise. Her eyes looked like jawbreakers after the colors had been sucked off.

"Wow," Bryan echoed, staring at Oscar. He shoved his hand back in his pocket. Empty. There was barely room for his hand, let alone a whole dog. Unless it was flattened, that is.

"You shouldn't stuff him in there, you might hurt him," Dad complained. Then he smiled. "But thanks, pal! Where was he?"

"Uh . . . out on the road," Bryan managed. He gestured vaguely toward the sky.

"Whew, good thing he didn't get flattened by a car!" Dad replied.

Spot sounded like she was choking on Rice Krispies. Bryan swallowed hard and elbowed her ribs.

Running his hand through Oscar's short hair, Dad added, "He seems okay, though."

The dog was more than okay, Bryan saw. Oscar squirmed toward his dog food, wagging his tail and drooling. Dad let him go, glancing up just in time to see Spot elbow Bryan in return.

"What are you two going on about?" Dad asked.

"Uh . . . uh . . . gotta go!" Spot spluttered.

Bryan caught her outside.

The words stuck in Spot's throat finally escaped. "He was flat! Not just knocked out!"

"Shhh. Tell me about it! But I can't say that to my dad."

"Flat!" Spot repeated. "Flat as a bookmark, flat as a—" She stopped. Her face wrinkled into a snarl. "Is this supposed to be funny? He was in your pocket the whole time, wasn't he?"

"No, Spot, honest. I don't—"

"Creep!" She shoved his shoulder. "I thought you might be my friend. I hope your new job stinks." She stuck out her tongue, whirled, and ran into the dark.

Bryan's head hurt. Maybe someone had played a trick on them both.

When he went back inside, Tripper offered him a strawberry shortcake. Dad already had a bowl in his lap. Dazed, Bryan just shook his head at her offer.

"Oh. Still not talking to me?" Tripper studied the floor. It wasn't true, but before he could think how to clear the muddle between them, she added, "Well, you're all safe, so I'm heading home. See you around."

Dad followed Tripper outside for a hug and possibly more. His father didn't need to miss his mom anymore, Bryan thought ruefully. Bryan still did.

Shaking off that uncomfortable idea, he grabbed Oscar. The dog wiggled away, but not before Bryan got a good feel of the bristly coat. It felt nothing like rubber. Bryan was pretty sure he could see a new line along Oscar's ribs, though, like a crease from a fold. The notion made his mind lurch. Ideas about ladies sawn in half and lizards that could grow back their tails tangled in his head. Unfortunately, none of those theories made much sense for a dog. Yet it couldn't be chance that he and Spot had found the flat Oscar just outside Acme's gate. The answer had to be related to Mr. Keen and whatever Trouble he planned to stir up.

His mind whirled all evening. Phone calls to a couple of friends turned up only an answering machine and a little sister. All Bryan could do was gather more clues for his pillowcase file. Several of the day's events would fit nicely in the envelope marked "Freaky," but he scrounged a separate one from Dad's office. He started to scribble "Acme" across the front. Realizing that more secrecy might be wise, he scratched out the *Ac* and wrote "Trouble" instead. By the time he hid the new envelope away, the margins of the meeting flyer inside were filled with notes like "impossibly flat dog"—not that Bryan would need a written reminder.

Uneasy, he waited until bedtime to bring up his new job. He hoped that by then Dad would be too tired to argue. Bryan felt a bit nervous about working for Mr. Keen, but that seemed like the best way to find out what was going on.

When his dad finally lowered the hydraulic lift, Bryan felt his heart speed up. He'd promised himself he couldn't put both feet under the covers without knowing what would happen in the morning. He gritted his teeth.

"Hey, Dad? I was wondering something." He dragged himself onto his bed. "If Oscar ever got really lost, would you offer a reward?"

His dad laughed. "If I thought it might help."

"Could you offer one this time?"

Dad's smiling eyes sharpened on Bryan. "What did you have in mind?"

Bryan couldn't breathe. He had to spit out the words jammed in his throat before they choked him.

"I got a job at Acme this evening, and I'm supposed to plant seeds in the morning, and I was hoping that, as a reward, you would let me."

Dad sat on the edge of the bed—not a good sign. "I've been thinking about that," he began. He tugged on Bryan's blanket. "I thought I might put in an application myself."

Bryan looked up from scrunching the sheets. "You?"

"You probably haven't noticed, but your dad's not getting rich pumping gas."

Bryan *had* noticed. That was why he had to save all his LemonMoo money—to buy for himself the computer his dad said they couldn't afford. Fewer cars pulled off the highway each week. He'd been afraid it would embarrass his father if he asked about it. From the look on Dad's face, he'd been right. Worse, Bryan had overheard enough fights to suspect that money had been one of the reasons his mother had left. It had been a long time, but he was still leery of poking old wounds.

"Tell you what, pal," Dad went on. "It sounds like you've made a commitment, so you need to keep it. We'll see how it goes. I might be able to keep an eye on you, anyhow."

"All right! Thanks!" Finally breathing again, Bryan grinned.

Dad clapped him on the shoulder. "Your first real job! I'm proud."

Bryan snuggled under the covers. Too excited to sleep, he stared at the ceiling and thought about Acme long after Dad had turned out the lights. The envelope marked "Trouble" seemed to hum through his pillow. The notes there didn't make sense yet, but if Bryan could figure out Mr. Keen's secret, he'd be the only one in South Wiggot who knew. No one else suspected, the dog's message had said. Either the Acme president was about to commit some crime or he had something juicy to hide.

Wishing he had a flashlight so he could add to his file, Bryan let his guesses run wild. Perhaps Mr. Keen made counterfeit money and used Acme as a fake front. Maybe he smuggled stolen goods in those big wooden crates. He might be in town to dig up buried loot from some bank heist or long-ago train robbery. This late at night, Bryan could even imagine the outlandish stranger greeting a ship full of aliens.

When the rumbling began, Bryan ignored it. Snores often buzzed around him at night.

Then the snow chains on the wall started to jingle.

"Pssst, Dad!" he called. "How about rolling over?"

Dad didn't budge. Bryan pulled off one sock, rolled it up, and aimed for his father's head. The bomb was lost in the growing roar. Every wrench and bolt in the garage rattled. Oscar jumped from Dad's bed and hid under a chair. Even Dad didn't snore *that* hard.

"Dad! Wake up! What's that noise?"

"Huh?" Dad lifted himself on one elbow, eyelids drooping.

"Is it an earthquake?" Bryan cried. "Or a UFO landing outside?"

Then the roar took a shape he recognized: *chugga-ta-CHUGGA-ta*. His bed shimmied in time to the beat. Feeling like a rag in a lopsided washing machine, he shouted, "It sounds like a—"

"Train, jus' a train," mumbled Dad. His face dropped back into his pillow. The roar seemed to follow. In seconds, the garage bay fell silent, except for soft snores.

Bryan whispered, "But there aren't any tracks around here."

8

TROUBLE WITH TOAST

In the bright morning sun, Bryan had to admit it: The train might have been the Dreamland Express. Dad's note didn't mention the nighttime disturbance. It said only, "Went to apply for that job. See you there? Dad."

Sticking out his tongue and blowing a rude noise through his lips, Bryan grabbed the bread sack propping up his dad's note. He hated eating breakfast alone. It made him think wistfully of ads on TV where kids sat at tables and moms poured glasses of orange juice.

The best remedy, he'd found, was to avoid being a

kid. Maybe he'd be a magician today. He dealt a few slices of bread onto the oversized toolchest that served as a table.

"Pick a card, any card," he told the eager audience in his head. "Remember your cards, please—and presto, they vanish!" He flipped two slices into the toaster and hit the button to make them disappear. While he waited for toast to pop up, he wondered how his dad would answer the questions on Mr. Keen's test.

Ka-chonk! Bryan reached for his tricky cards. Toasted bread rose from one slot. An actual white card poked out of the other.

"Whoa!" Bryan grabbed the card, afraid it might flame up. One edge was charred. "Ow, hot."

It was not a playing card, in fact, but an envelope with his name printed on top. Bryan stared at it. His dad sometimes tossed screwdrivers into the silverware drawer, but he would never put mail in the toaster!

A shiver ran across Bryan's skin. He was certain no paper had poked from the slot when he'd dropped his bread in. Afraid something more scary might pop out next, he yanked the power cord from the wall and stuffed the toaster into the fridge.

Bryan returned to prod his toaster-gram with his

fork. Then he remembered that mail was Tripper's specialty. She probably knew lots of post office tricks.

"All right, apology accepted. Geez," Bryan said. He tore open the envelope.

It wasn't from Tripper after all.

"Eat a good breakfast," the note inside read. "Nibbling by planters is strictly forbidden. K."

"K for Keen, Master of Mystery?" Bryan wondered aloud. At his voice, the note vanished with a firecracker *POP!* The envelope followed with a weak sizzle. Nothing was left but the odor of onions.

"Ha! Cool!" Bryan cried. He felt like part of a spy ring. Then the onion smell began stinging his eyes. He grabbed his dry toast and ran out.

Before he'd passed the last gas pump, Bryan realized how it would sound to anyone else. Pop-up toaster mail? Self-destruct notes? Not to mention foldable dogs. If Dad didn't think he was feverish and put him to bed, he'd at least put the kibosh on Bryan's job. All the mystery pointed to one thing: Acme was up to no good. He'd best stay quiet, pretend nothing was odd, and keep his eyes open for traps. He could work undercover until he could amaze everyone with the truth.

He'd have to be careful, of course. He liked

Mr. Keen, but there was no way he could trust him. For all Bryan knew, the strange man was part of an alien invasion preparing to conquer South Wiggot. Forget *Crookbusters*—a story like that might even get Bryan an interview with the president!

He ran back inside and added a few notes to his pillowcase file:

> Mail in the toaster (secret technology?)
> Spies?
> Invaders from another country—or
>   another planet!!

Ready to help save the earth, Bryan arrived for work at 9 A.M. sharp. He was startled to find Spot in the gatehouse.

"What are you doing here?" he asked.

She pointed to a tag on her shirt that read ACME SECURITY. "Grrr . . . wow-wow-wow!" A two-legged guard dog, she snapped her teeth at him.

"I get it," he said, backing up. He wondered if Spot had known the answer to "How many eggs in a year?" Something teetered inside his chest. Maybe he wasn't so special after all. Then again, security guards probably took a different test. And she might be in a good position to help him.

He stuck out his hand. "Congratulations."

She gazed at his hand doubtfully.

"Listen, Spot," he said. "I don't know how Oscar got flat. No fooling. There's something weird going on." He searched the gatehouse eaves for a spy camera, then whispered, "Don't forget that note on the Saint Bernard. We're the only ones who saw it, so we ought to stick together." Thrusting his hand out again, he added, "Shake, girl, shake!"

Spot giggled and slapped Bryan's palm. Relieved, he gave her a slap back.

"Keep an eye out for anything suspicious," he said.

She sniffed left and right like a bloodhound and finished with a fast thumbs-up.

Glad to have an ally, even if she was odd, Bryan waved and hurried toward the Acme office—and whatever lurked behind its three colored doors.

Mr. Keen met him on the doorstep.

"Superb," the man said, checking his watch. "And not a second too soon for the stomping to start. Follow me." He strode toward the corner of the building.

Intrigued, Bryan followed. They passed several trucks at the loading dock. Inside the dim trailers, townsfolk filled out job applications. A stranger handed out pencils and forms. He or she—there was no way to tell—wore swollen white coveralls, booties and gloves, and a helmet with a face mask that shone like a mirror.

Bryan stopped in his tracks. "Is that a space suit?"

More white-clad figures arrived with armloads of painting supplies. They looked like Stormtroopers from a lost Star Wars movie called *The Empire Gets Fat*.

"No and more no," said Mr. Keen, barely slowing. "Whatever gave you that thought?"

Bryan pointed. "It looks like they're ready to blast off. Or defuse a bomb."

"Oh, that. Standard uniform. For painting," Mr. Keen added. "Scientifically designed to repel splashes and drips. Snappy, aren't they?"

Sure, if you like the Pillsbury Doughboy, Bryan thought. He shuddered. He'd have to see someone with no helmet to be convinced they were human.

Among the others Bryan spotted Joelle and Bettina, the hog-farming sisters who had once babysat him, and a couple of teenagers who usually worked at the feed store. He did not, however, see his father. Maybe Dad was already inside one of those creepy suits. Glad he was a planter and not a painter, Bryan caught up with Mr. Keen.

He smelled it before he saw it: Fresh popcorn steam wafted around the corner. A popping cart sat at the rear of the building, kernels merrily bouncing inside. Mr. Keen scooped the white puffs into a five-gallon bucket and handed it over.

Bryan grinned. The delicious aroma reminded him that he'd skipped most of his breakfast. He grabbed a fistful of corn.

It never reached his lips.

9

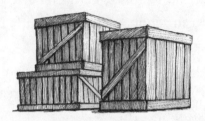

SOWING ODD SEED

Mr. Keen jabbed the air with a finger as sharp as an ice pick. Bryan suddenly remembered his toaster note: No nibbling. The tender popcorn tumbled back out of his palm.

After a glare that would wither plastic flowers, the Acme chief bent his long body until his face nearly touched the ground.

"Watch closely, please."

The field had been freshly plowed into cocoa-brown rows. "First, poke a hole," Mr. Keen said. "Pinkies preferred." His right pinkie plunged into the soil. He stuffed a single piece of popcorn into the hole. "One pinkie, one seed."

He looked up to make sure his new employee was watching. Trying to keep a straight face, Bryan shifted the bucket in his arms.

"Question?" Mr. Keen demanded.

"I don't think you can plant popcorn that's already popped," Bryan said carefully. He didn't want to get fired. He'd already nearly broken the only rule he knew. "To grow popcorn you'd have to plant it while it's still, uh, corny."

"Who said anything about growing popcorn? Watch. After sowing, you stomp." Mr. Keen's white

shoe mashed the dirt so it buried the popcorn. "Poke, sow, stomp. Simple as that." He gestured for Bryan to try it.

"Won't it just rot?" Bryan asked. "If you're not trying to grow popcorn, what do you think will sprout?"

"Acme's cash crop, of course. If you want to grow poofs, you have to plant something poofy, now don't you?"

Bryan looked doubtfully into the bucket. Mr. Keen might not be a bad guy or spy after all. He might just be a nut. In a week or two, when nothing had sprouted, would planters still get paid?

"Don't worry, I haven't forgotten your wages."

Bryan jumped, unnerved that his boss had just read his mind.

"How about ten dollars an hour," continued Mr. Keen, "paid at the end of each day?"

It sounded too good to be true. Then Bryan remembered the gold coins.

"Real dollar bills?"

Mr. Keen rolled his eyes. "Dollars or pieces of seven, it's up to you."

"Dollars, please." Bryan stuck his smallest finger into the dirt, stuffed in a choice bit of popcorn, and squashed his heel on top.

"A bit more stomp—the stomping's the secret."

Bryan stepped again, harder. "Am I the only planter?" he wondered.

"For now. We'll see how you do."

Piece by piece, Bryan stuffed popcorn into the ground. It seemed like a terrible waste. Someone who could send mail through the toaster, however, could not be too crazy. The popcorn must be a cover for something more sinister. Bryan couldn't see anything fishy from here in the field, though, and the back of the factory was blank. Only a big metal Dumpster crouched near the far corner.

Eventually, he emptied his bucket. When he went to refill it, he checked out the Dumpster. Nothing lurked inside but a few bags that had once held unpopped popcorn. The popper looked ordinary, too, except that one wheel was flat.

He tried to recall every word in the Saint Bernard's note. The lines had included "The locals don't seem to suspect." One local—Bryan—suspected something, all right, but he didn't know what. Lots of things seemed suspicious.

He decided he could rule out counterfeiting, smuggling, or any other crime where the factory was just there for a fake front. Nobody would believe that a business planting popped corn was honest. Local cops would be sniffing around all the time. So unless Mr. Keen was a lousy crook, there had to be something else behind his confusing behavior.

While he puzzled, Bryan planted enough popcorn for a whole movie theater. When his stomach began growling, he had to pretend the white bits were Styrofoam beans. He wished he'd remembered a lunch.

The sun was thumping the top of his head when Spot came around the corner with a lunch sack.

"Woof," she said in hello. "It's lunchtime. Wanna sit together to eat?"

"I didn't bring anything," he admitted. "I wonder if I have time to run home."

"Want half of my sandwich instead?"

"Is it dog food?"

"Almost. It's meatloaf." She pulled it out. The thick slab of meat and grainy bread looked delicious. Bryan accepted her offer, and they sat together in the building's cool shadow.

They mused about his strange duties, and Spot spent a few minutes naming townsfolk she'd seen donning suits, hauling paint, or passing back out through the gate. Then they fell silent.

Once his half of the sandwich was gone, Bryan risked a snoopy question.

"So what's with the dog stuff?" He licked bits of

meatloaf from his fingers and tried not to covet Spot's apple as well.

She lowered her head. "If I tell you, will you still talk to me?"

"Sure," Bryan replied. "It's not like it's contagious."

"I guess not," she said. Before he could respond, she pulled at her top lip with one finger to show him her upper teeth. A few were so pointed they looked like plastic Halloween fangs. Bryan tried not to recoil.

"I have these two extra teeth," she explained. "The pointy ones—canines, they're called." Her voice dropped. "Sooner or later, the rest of my canine genes will switch on. I'll get all hairy and grow a tail and turn into a dog."

"Come off it," Bryan said, when he realized she meant it. "Who told you that?"

"My uncle," she replied. "He should know. He was born with a little tail that the doctors whacked off. The hospitals try to keep stuff like that quiet, but it's true."

Speechless, Bryan remembered hearing just that odd fact on TV: A small percentage of people came into the world with a tail. It had never occurred to him that it had happened to anyone in South Wiggot.

"It's called hounditis," Spot continued, "and it runs in the family. I guess my uncle was cured when

71

they chopped off his tail, or at least he hasn't turned into a dog yet. But my aunt, who's into astrology, checked my star charts for my entire life. She discovered that I was born under the Dog Star with a comet in Canis Major. So my horoscope predicts I'll go doggy, too."

Bryan snorted, his skepticism returning. "And you believe it?"

Spot poked her thumbnail through the skin of her apple, then shrugged. "I've got these teeth, don't I? My whole family talks about it. And my cousin Grace is a poodle. She eats at the table and everything."

Almost certain that Spot's family was pulling her leg, Bryan hardly knew what to say. He'd seen some strange photos on the covers of grocery store tabloids, but he thought everyone knew they were phony. Here was someone who expected to appear there herself someday.

"Even if it's true and you get really hairy or something," he ventured, feeling sorry for her, "it might not happen for years. Why not be a person as long as you can?"

"I started to worry I might change all at once," she explained, "and nobody would know it was me. I figured if I wear a dog collar and all that, when I finally turn doggy, people could still recognize me—and not chase me off because they think I'm some stray." Her face crumpled and she murmured, "I don't want to end up in the dog pound, abandoned."

Abandoned. That word gave Bryan an unexpected twinge for his absent mother. He thought he understood how Spot felt.

"Except for that," she added, regaining her calm, "it isn't so bad. At least dogs are loyal and friendly and always happy."

"Some people are, too," he protested weakly.

Spot eyed him. "Name one."

Bryan faltered. Tripper came to mind. In some ways his dad's boisterous girlfriend was more doglike than Spot. He wasn't entirely comfortable with that thought, perhaps because it led to another: Tripper was nothing like his mother, and that was both reassuring and hurtful at the same time.

Giving up on getting an answer, Spot said, "Besides, I want to be someone's best friend."

Bryan pressed the tip of his tongue between his lips and kept quiet. He knew what Spot hoped he would say, but he wasn't sure he wanted to say it. She was a girl, after all, and younger than he was, and she pretended that she was a dog.

She gathered up her lunch trash soon after.

"See ya," she sighed. "I better go back to the guardhouse."

"Thanks for the sandwich. And for coming around."

With effort, she managed a smile.

The planting continued. Despite Spot's generosity, by late afternoon Bryan was starving. Mr. Keen had warned him again before leaving, "Nibbling is grounds for dismissal." Bryan resisted temptation. When he returned to the popper for another load, though, the warm aroma fuzzied his head. He reached into the fluffy kernels. Would anyone really notice if he swiped just a handful or two?

An alarm shrieked. Bryan jerked his hand from the popper. Mr. Keen appeared from nowhere. The man's narrow eyes seemed to bore straight through Bryan to spot any illegal popcorn inside his stomach. When that stare switched to a grin, the alarm screeched to a halt.

"Quitting time. How far did you get?"

Ready to apologize for even *thinking* about nibbling, Bryan pointed out his last, distant row.

"Excellent stomping. Here is your pay." Crisp ten-dollar bills slid from Mr. Keen's sleeve. He counted them out. Then he crumpled each into a nugget and poured the nuggets into Bryan's palm.

"Just a reminder. At Acme, popcorn equals pay. Don't eat either one."

"Yes, sir—I mean, no, sir—I won't."

Relieved, Bryan ran home, his wages bouncing between his cupped hands. He hadn't learned any Acme secrets yet, but he felt rich.

The gas station office was empty. Panting, Bryan pulled his money can from the shelf. He almost dropped it. It weighed at least twice as much as he remembered. He popped off the plastic lid. The scent of old coffee mingled with the sharp tang of coins. Quarters and dimes swam cheerfully together, with a dollar bill poking out here and there. In the center rested his gold pieces of seven.

"Wow," Bryan breathed. There weren't that many coins in the can yesterday! He stirred the silver. It felt slithery, like a can full of beetles. Maybe Dad or Tripper had added some coins as a surprise, but they couldn't have given him this many.

The gold coins winked. Mr. Keen had said they were lucky. Lucky, indeed! Bryan hooted. Who needed to make counterfeit money when it could multiply by itself? He was onto something big.

He uncrimped today's pay. The crumpled bills looked tired compared to the glittering coins. Still, maybe there would be double the dollars tomorrow. Smirking, Bryan dropped them into the can. Then he turned all the top coins on their heads. If anyone slipped in more, the new coins would disturb the pattern.

Proud of his booby trap, Bryan jigged toward the doorway. Before he reached it, an idea halted him. Slowly he turned to gaze at the file cabinet. The first two drawers held gas station paperwork. The third drawer contained things his father needed as mayor, although Bryan had never bothered to look at them. Nothing about garbage collection, taxes, or council meetings could possibly interest him.

A contract for the lease of the TaterNugget plant, on the other hand, might.

10

A PLUNGE AND
A PUZZLE

The metal drawer opened with the slightest tug. Heat flooded Bryan's skin as he stared at the files.

His curiosity overcame his conscience. Once he'd made the plunge to snoop, his fingers moved quickly. A photocopy of the Acme contract had been tucked in a folder marked "Real Estate." He riffled through pages packed with legal mumbo jumbo like "whereas" and "henceforth."

The last page contained most of the good stuff. Bryan didn't care how much Acme paid for the lease or how long it would last, either, until he saw this: "For the period of one year, unless the world ends before then (through the actions of Acme representatives or anyone else), in which case this contract will become null and void. Not responsible for global chaos or mass hysteria."

Bryan reread those lines. He didn't think his dad's paperwork usually included anything about the end of the world. This hinted that Acme might cause it. That qualified as Trouble, all right.

He scanned the rest of the page, disappointed to find nothing about where Acme or its president had come from. The only other interesting tidbit appeared beneath a scribble that must have been Mr. Keen's signature. A line of fine print there read, "Archibald Keen, DDS, official I^5 representative of Acme Inc. No resemblance to persons living or dead is intended." Bryan had never seen those last words anywhere but at the end of a movie.

Feeling as if it were all a little unreal, he stuffed the papers back into the folder and slammed the drawer.

Before he left his dad's office, Bryan pulled out the dictionary he sometimes needed for homework. He found two possibilities for the *DDS* after Mr. Keen's name. It was hard to believe that the newcomer might be a dentist, but Dandelion Development Specialist wasn't much better. There was no entry at all for I^5.

Of course, the dictionary didn't list the square root of *H*, either.

His pillowcase file needed an update. On a new sheet of paper, Bryan copied his old notes more neatly and added many more. When he was done, the sheet looked like this:

Impossibly flat dog
Mail in the toaster (secret technology?)
Arrived in a crate
Gold coins
Invaders from another country—or
    another planet!
Note sent on a Saint Bernard
Explosions during the meeting

Acme stands for Astro-Chrono-Magical
    Enterprises

Spies?
Eggteen
Clock in the ceiling
Railroad noise without train tracks
Employees have to wear creepy white suits
Ten dollars an hour for planting popped
    popcorn!

Archibald Keen, D.D.S. (dentist or
    dandelion specialist?)
Global chaos or mass hysteria
End of the world in the contract
No resemblance to persons living or dead
Trouble with a capital T

Bryan read down the list to make sure he hadn't left anything off. It looked like a lot of clues, but if they added up, he sure didn't see how. Baffled, he hid the file away.

Since Dad hadn't appeared and the kitchen contained no sign of dinner, Bryan rummaged for a snack. Cheese or a pickle? He was standing before the refrigerator trying to choose when someone banged on the office door. *Bam, bam, bam!* Before he could move, footsteps raced through the office toward him.

Bryan grabbed the only weapon within reach—a two-liter bottle of cola.

11

A MICE CUP OF TEA

If he shook the soda pop hard enough, Bryan thought wildly, it might squirt into the intruder's eyes and give him a chance to run away.

"Rich! Where are you?" Tripper dashed in and slid to a halt. Her long hair whipped as she whirled her head, searching. Dust and burrs clung to the bed slippers she wore with her T-shirt and shorts. She clutched a teakettle in one hand and a small box of teabags in the other.

Bryan would have laughed—if only she'd been joking around. With her eyes popping, Tripper looked even more scared than he was.

"He's not here. What's wrong?"

"Listen to this," Tripper said. "Give me a cup."

Bryan returned the soda to the refrigerator. After yesterday's fight, he didn't like being ordered around, but curiosity nudged him to obey. He found her a mug, set it down, and backed away.

She poured water from her teakettle into the cup, took a teabag, and dunked it.

"EEEEeeeeeeee!" the teabag squealed. Tripper yanked it back out of the water.

"Hear that?" she demanded.

It wasn't a teabag after all. It was a mouse, caught by the tail in Tripper's fingers.

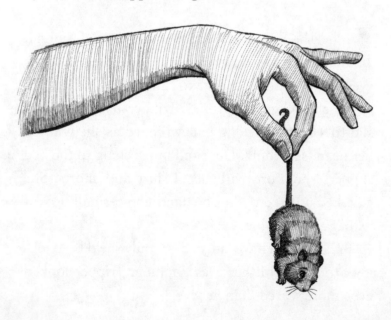

"What are you doing?" Bryan cried, plucking the poor mouse from her grip. "You'll drown him!" The creature cowered in his palm, black eyes blinking, water dribbling off its fur.

"You can't drown a teabag. But they're not supposed to make noise!"

"Are you blind? It's not a teabag. It's a mouse!"

"Don't be ridiculous," Tripper snapped. "It's a Nice-n-Spice teabag. But it's the third one that screamed." She slapped her hands over her face and sank into a chair. "I must be losing my mind."

Scared she might be right, Bryan stared at her, unsure how she could possibly mistake the mouse for a teabag, even if its hairless tail did resemble a string.

"Look," he said. "Don't you believe your own eyes?"

She peered into his cupped hand. "All I see is a teabag. Slightly damp. If you see something else, one of us is in trouble."

The word *trouble* reminded Bryan of Mr. Keen and the odd noises from Acme's office door yesterday.

"Close your eyes," he told Tripper, inspired. "Stick out your hand." Her face screwed up in doubt, she complied. Her fingers shook.

Bryan set the mouse in her palm. The little creature took two steps toward Tripper's wrist—two too many. She yelped. Her hand jerked. The mouse dropped to the floor and scurried away.

"It *is* a mouse! I felt its little feet! Yeeeeeeeeeooooo—"

"Tripper! Stop!"

Her eyes flew open. She breathed in great gulps. He'd never seen an adult look so frightened except on TV. It made him want to run, too.

"It's okay," Bryan said. He wasn't sure it was true, but it made him feel better. "He must have crawled into your cupboard looking for crumbs."

"Three. Three," she repeated. "The whole box can't be mice, can it?" She thrust it at Bryan.

He didn't have to open it. He could tell by the scratching inside. "It feels like it," he said.

She lifted the flap. Amazingly, none of the six or seven mice there leapt out. Instead they froze, twitching their noses. Bryan braced for another screech from Tripper.

"One, two, three . . . seven. Seven teabags," she counted.

He raised his eyes from the mice to Tripper's face. "You really can't see the mice?"

"I really can't." She closed her eyes again, wrapping her hands around the box. "But I can feel them

wiggling." Her voice wound up like a straining trac-
tor engine. "Take 'em! Before I scream again!"

Bryan carried the mice outside. The moment he set
the box on the dirt, they jumped in all directions. Once
the tea box sat empty, the last few minutes began to
feel like a dream. He returned inside, thoughtful.

Tripper was muttering to herself. "Migraine
headache. They say you see things with those. Or . . .
hmm." She stared into the distance. "The explosions
yesterday. Toxic waste. Radiation. That could goof
up my vision, sure."

"They all ran away," Bryan told her. "Are you all
right?"

Tripper heaved a sigh. "I don't think so." Nonethe-
less, she rose to her feet. "I'm going home. I'll lie
down and figure out what to do in the morning."
Before she left, she added, "Ask your dad to call me,
will you?"

Bryan's father returned home not much later. He
was holding a take-out pizza.

"Sorry, pal," he said. "Had some mayor stuff at
the county office, and it took more time than I
planned."

The aroma of warm cheese hit Bryan. His stomach moaned. He was halfway through his second

piece of pizza before he stopped chewing long enough to speak.

"Tripper wants you to call her. She had mice in her tea." The words sounded strange enough in his own ears to stop him. He added, "She was pretty upset."

Dad rubbed his chin. "I'm sure I can fix a little problem like that."

Don't bet on it, Bryan thought, nipping at a pepperoni slice. He would let Tripper handle the details, though. She hadn't exactly done him any favors lately.

"I didn't see you at Acme today," he said instead. "Didn't you get a job, Dad?"

His father's face sagged. "They wouldn't hire me. False teeth." With his tongue, Dad clacked his dentures. Most of his real teeth had been knocked out by a skateboard years ago. "They called it a safety hazard."

Bryan stretched a blob of cheese between his fingers. He felt sorry for his dad, but a rush of pride also warmed him. It wasn't every day he could do something Dad couldn't. His father liked to say they were partners. For once Bryan felt it was true.

Dad pulled on a smile. "So how was work, pal? No safety hazards for you, right?"

"Safe as dirt," Bryan said. "I got paid already, too." He resolved to give Dad half of his wages. If he wasn't smart enough to figure out Mr. Keen's secrets, he could at least pay some of their bills like a real partner.

He described his day stomping seeds. Astonishment twisted Dad's face.

"I guess we'd better keep an eye on that place. It sounds like baloney to me."

"Nah, baloney seeds are bigger," Bryan joked. "I hope it sprouts candy corn."

"It might look like you planted bird seed." Dad grinned. "I bet your field will be covered with hungry crows in the morning."

"Pop-caw'n?" Bryan giggled. They made other corny jests all evening. After his weird workday and the even stranger visit by Tripper, the hours before bedtime felt cozy and normal. Bryan was glad to have his dad to himself. When he finally crawled into bed, he did not take the time to add anything to the file concealed in his pillow.

12

TRIPPED UP

No trains disturbed Bryan's sleep that night. He rolled over once to hear a far-off squealing like fingertips stroking a balloon, but he'd heard stranger things in his dad's snores before.

When he climbed down from bed the next morning, a pot of oatmeal awaited, hot and ready for milk. Dad was already bent over paperwork in his office. Hoping the file cabinet didn't show any sign of his snooping, Bryan filled his bowl. He skipped the spoon, slurping his breakfast through a fat straw like a giant mush-sucking mosquito. Then he made two cream cheese sandwiches with plenty of jelly, wrapped them in aluminum foil, and stuffed them into his shirt.

After collecting a hug from his father, he headed for work. Halfway there, Bryan made a quick detour to knock on the back door of the post office. The rear of the building held the small apartment Tripper called home.

When she answered, she took a step back as if expecting him to explode.

"Bryan. Oh, boy."

Her unwelcoming tone wiped away his plans for being polite. He asked, "What did my dad say about the mice?"

"I haven't talked to him." She squirmed uncomfortably. "Did you?"

"I told him to call you. I didn't exactly say why."

Tripper sank down to sit on the threshold. "Good," she replied. At his puzzled look, she added, "Maybe you haven't noticed, Bryan, but . . . I like your dad a lot."

"Duh. You're his girlfriend, aren't you?" Bryan faltered, surprised by the longing those words sent swirling inside him. But he reminded himself that a girlfriend and a mother were two different things.

Tripper had covered her mouth with her hand. Now she removed it to speak again.

"There must be some good reason I couldn't see those mice. Until I can explain it, I'd rather not say anything to your dad. I don't want him to decide I'm a kook."

"You are a kook," Bryan said. "What's that got to do with it?"

With a wry twist of her lips, she added, "Okay then, I don't want him to think I'm too paranoid about that new factory he's so proud of."

Behind his eyeballs, Bryan's brain calculated overtime. Should he tell her about all the mysterious things he'd seen and heard lately? After the mice, she'd probably believe him. She might even be able to help. Then again, she might haul him straight to his dad and insist they call the police or leave town or—

"What?" she wondered, spotting his uncertainty. Her face folded in suspicion. "Wait a minute. You didn't do something to get even with me, did you?"

Bryan choked. "Like what?" he demanded. "Even if I *had* put mice in your cupboard, how could I make you see teabags instead?"

Tripper sagged like a week-old balloon. "I don't know. Gas in my LemonMoo?" She tugged her long hair. "Oh, I know you wouldn't do *that*. But . . ."

Bryan stomped the dust. He'd been feeling sorry

for her until then. Now she sounded like Spot, accusing him of dirty tricks. His hunch had been right. He couldn't trust her. He couldn't trust anyone.

"Wait. You started your job yesterday, right?" Tripper asked. "What did you see? Chemicals? Big oozing vats?"

Bryan clamped his jaw. He supposed there *could* be toxic waste in the factory or the truck trailers, though. Relenting, he shook his head.

"Nothing like that," he grumbled. "But the people who paint wear these space suits."

"Aha." Tripper got to her feet. "I might have to do a little research."

"Have they gotten any mail?" Bryan wondered.

"Not yet. I'd expect it to take a few days, though." Catching the idea that had prompted his question, she shook her head. "Oh, no, don't even think about it. Tampering with mail is a big crime."

"Who said anything about tampering?" Bryan protested, glad he hadn't mentioned his peek at the contract. "Just see where it comes from. And where it goes, if they send any." He doubted they would.

"Hmm." Scowling, Tripper rubbed her lips with her fingers.

"I gotta go," Bryan told her. He'd had enough disapproval.

Her face cramped in concern. "I wish you weren't going back there."

Bryan plunked his hands on his hips.

"I know, I know," Tripper added. She raised her palms in surrender. "Just be careful."

As he hurried on to work, Bryan felt his belly churn. Maybe he should have told Tripper more. Still, he didn't see how any kind of pollution could put letters in toasters or make your dachshund collapsible. Tripper just thought she knew everything.

The more he considered it, the more she felt like competition. He couldn't let her figure it out before he did. He strode through the factory gate more determined than ever.

The Acme guardhouse was empty. Bryan hurried toward the field to see if Spot or any other new seed stompers worked there. As he turned the corner, a golden glare hit his eyes. He gaped. Dandelion blooms by the million bobbed on a sea of green leaves.

"Oh, no!" His shoulders drooped. Bryan had never seen so many weeds. He'd probably have to pull them, and he hated that chore. How did they take over so fast? There certainly had been no baby weeds in the dirt yesterday.

A breeze combed the stems. The weeds waved in rows as if they'd been planted. Frowning, Bryan stepped closer. He knew where dandelions came from, and it was *not* from popped corn. Then his ears caught a squeak. He'd heard it before. Near his feet, a green tendril squealed from the earth, unfurled, and popped open a yellow umbrella.

The skin on Bryan's neck crawled. Surrounded by an army of weeds, he backed away slowly. What if they pulled their roots from the ground and attacked?

The big yellow blooms glared right at him.

13

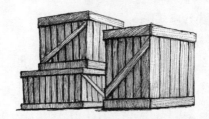

A DISTURBING
DENTIST

Bryan ran. He got as far as the corner of the building before he stopped. Were a bunch of weeds scaring him off? What if every Crookbuster got scared and ran? The weeds were extra healthy, sure. They were short, though, and they didn't even have thorns. What were they going to do, bite his ankles? Tripper was making him paranoid, that's all. Feeling foolish, Bryan marched to the Acme office.

As he reached for the door, Spot jumped out, slamming into him.

"Hey," he complained, barely keeping on his feet. Jelly from his sandwiches oozed into his shirt.

"Sorry." She dodged.

Wham! Bouncing off somebody else, Spot tripped and fell to her knees. The other person, who was wearing one of those spooky white suits, lifted her up, brushed her off, and herded them both into the office. The door shut behind them.

Townsfolk dozed in chairs around the small room. Someone had begun a fresh coat of paint on one wall. Except for the paint smell, Bryan couldn't see what might have made Spot run.

Then the room's blue door gave way. Pastor Daniels stepped out, one palm cupping his jaw.

"Hewwo," he said, giving Bryan and Spot a lop-sided smile. He shook hands with Mr. Keen, who wore a white lab coat. A magnifying glass was suspended from the Acme chief's forehead. That *DDS* on the contract—he really was a dentist!

"The numbness will wear off soon," Mr. Keen told the pastor. "Thank you for coming to Free Dental Work Day." As Pastor Daniels left, Mr. Keen turned his searchlight smile onto Bryan.

"No planting today," he explained. "Today is for teeth. Caps, root canals, fillings—whatever you need. Have a seat."

Spot growled. Mr. Keen ushered the next person toward the blue door.

"I never need fillings," Bryan said. "The Lemon-Moo takes care of that."

"Nonsense. Everyone needs a filling or two!" The blue door closed with a click.

Spot sagged against the wall, fidgeting with her dog collar.

"Scared of the dentist?" Bryan asked. After seeing her teeth yesterday, he figured she had a pretty good reason to stay away from someone with pliers at hand.

She only whined.

"Don't worry. Pastor Daniels would have warned us of anything funky." Bryan lowered his voice. "You want something creepy, I can do better than the dentist. Mutant dandelions, out behind the factory. They're growing so fast you can—"

Someone hammered on the front door. Mr. Keen returned to the lobby to answer. A handful of farmers stood outside, their thumbs curled around the straps of their overalls.

"Howdy. Hope we're not interrupting," said a man Bryan knew as the main supplier of LemonMoo milk. "We came to ask you to do sumpin' about your weed problem."

"I'm not aware of a weed problem," replied Mr. Keen.

"Your back lot. It's a menace to our fields," said the man who grew alfalfa next door. "Burn those dandelions before they go to seed. Or we will." He banged his boot against the doorframe.

"Is that what you're worried about? Oh, ho ho," Mr. Keen responded. Visions of tall, skinny Santas gave Bryan a shiver. "Ho ho hee. I assure you, not a single seed shall drift away. See me next week if I'm wrong."

The farmers grumbled. "We'll do that, thanks," said the polite one.

"And drop by later for your free dental checkup!" Mr. Keen closed the door. He caught Bryan's eye. "Nincompoops," he muttered. His lab coat flapped as he hurried back behind the blue door.

"See?" Bryan turned to Spot. She was gone.

He scanned the room. Nothing moved. Even the clock fan in the ceiling hung still. As he watched, though, the minute hand jerked ten minutes.

He looked around again. A shoestring stuck out from beneath a yellow door. Bryan wasn't a shoestring expert, but he guessed that Spot must be hiding on the other side of that door.

He crept over, turned the knob, and slipped in.

Spot skittered away on all fours like a spider.

Before Bryan's eyes could focus on the room, a fat white arm reached over his shoulder to grab him.

"Yikes!" He jumped away. Spot giggled, then slapped her hand over her mouth. Whirling, Bryan saw his mistake. Behind the door, a half-dozen empty Acme uniforms dangled from hooks. The mirrored helmets flopped to one side, making the suits look like zombies with broken necks. Bryan shuddered.

While Spot tied her shoe, he scanned the room. Coils of vacuum hose spilled from one corner. Another held a mound of what looked like albino bagpipes. Hammers and paintbrushes were piled near gallons of Acme paint labeled ANY COLOR MADE EASY.

Since there was no way out except through the lobby, Spot tried to bury herself under the vacuum hose. As she wrestled with coils, one of her feet kicked a small, golden lump across the floor. Bryan picked up what turned out to be a dusty and rock-hard TaterNugget. Though practically a fossil, it still smelled of hot oil.

A new theory popped into Bryan's head. Mr. Keen may have arrived from the future! Someone who could travel through time would be loaded with great technology. Mutant dandelions and shape-shifting teabags might be commonplace in 2020 or so. He stuffed his find into his pocket to add to his file.

Spot had given up hiding except to wrap her arms over her head.

"Listen, Spot," Bryan said. He moved closer so he could whisper. "Mr. Keen might be scary, but not because he's a dentist."

Her face made it clear she didn't agree. "What kind of dentist runs a factory?" she hissed. "A demented one, maybe!"

"Well, at first I thought he must be a crook. But Acme's too weird for any ordinary crime. He can't be a spy, either, unless real secret agents get even better gadgets than the ones in the movies." Bryan reconsidered how the hoses and bagpipes might be used.

"Did you see anything suspicious from the guardhouse yesterday?" he asked.

The uncertain gleam in Spot's eyes suggested the answer was yes, but her pigtails flew as her head shook.

"I bet he's a mad scientist," she said.

That possibility had not occurred to Bryan. Wishing he could make notes for his file, he jotted Spot's idea in the dust on the floor, since writing it now would help him remember it later. Scrunching his face and thinking hard, he added a few more:

Inventor or maD scientist
dEmented dentist
Alien
Spy Or coUnterspy
Time traveler frOm the Future
Hypnotist
Evil genius
amAzing wizarD (for real)
Superhero

"We might need a superhero to figure it out," Bryan sighed.

"You put capital letters in the middle of some of the words." Spot pointed.

He saw what she meant. He hadn't done it on purpose, but there they were. Feeling like a dunce, he wiped the dust writing away.

"Wait!" She grabbed his wrist too late. Her face fell. "It could have been a sign. Like a Ouija board spelling things out by itself."

Bryan scoffed. "Whatever he is, he isn't a ghost."

"How do you know? I liked the alien idea best, though."

That explanation fit his mishmash of clues as well as any, he had to admit. He got up and inspected the uniforms on the wall to see if they might really be space suits.

"I don't know if anything like this has happened to you," he began, "but yesterday—"

The yellow door flew open.

14

MOUTHS LEFT UNMUFFLED

The door knocked Bryan into the white suits behind it. Recovering his balance, he rubbed his banged shoulder.

"There you are, Spot! Your turn for tidy teeth!" Unaware that Bryan was behind the door, Mr. Keen stepped in. "I should scold you for snooping," he added, urging her toward the doorway, "but I suppose my security guard should know what she's guarding, eh?"

Not sure his boss would feel the same about a snooping seed stomper, Bryan ducked behind the nearest white suit. He poked his head and arms into the unzipped slit running up the back of the uniform. Scared he'd be seen when Mr. Keen turned around, he also lifted in one leg so it wouldn't stick out like Spot's shoelace. Light shone through tiny air holes in the suit's armpit. After a test sniff, Bryan shoved his face there to peek out. Through the holes he watched Spot drag her heels toward the lobby.

"Have no fear, my dear Spot," Mr. Keen said. "We'll be done in a flash." He spun toward the suits.

Bryan froze even his eyeballs.

"Bring a child-sized Anti-Cavity Mouth Examiner, please."

Something shifted under Bryan's left foot. To his horror, one clunky boot beneath him took a step. A sleeve slapped the helmet into place. Strangled by panic, Bryan fell forward into the stiff outfit as it stepped again. His right leg dragged behind like a tail. When the zipper in the back of the suit began to clack, Bryan yanked his right foot inside, too—he didn't want his leg zipped off!

The suit reached for an item on a shelf, then followed Mr. Keen. Breathless, Bryan wobbled around inside, too short to see out through the face mask. Sweat popped into the crooks of his elbows while his fingers fumbled for the zipper. He found he could grab the zipper pull and undo it, so he wouldn't be trapped. He didn't want to get caught climbing out, though. He'd wait for a chance when no one could see.

Fortunately, when the suit raised its arms—as it did to open the door—Bryan could peek out the armpit. The people in the lobby barely glanced up as he passed. If only they knew! There weren't employees inside the white suits; they were robots! This one seemed to respond to Mr. Keen's voice. Bryan wondered if the robot would obey commands from inside. He was too scared of making any noise to find out.

The smell of drilled teeth seeped into his nose. Dental equipment crowded the room behind the blue door. X-ray pictures of South Wiggot teeth hung on the walls.

"Have a seat," Mr. Keen suggested, snapping fresh latex gloves onto his hands. Spot crossed her arms but didn't otherwise move. "Stand if you prefer, then," he continued. "This part won't take a minute."

Bryan's suit handed Mr. Keen a corkscrew device that looked like a cross between a skinny flashlight and a carrot that had coiled around a rock as it grew. Mr. Keen had gripped a similar tool when he'd climbed out of the crate on the highway.

"Our exclusive Anti-Cavity Mouth Examiner, the latest in dental detection," Mr. Keen told Spot. He fiddled with the device. Light flashed from its tip. "It finds tooth decay, wisdom teeth, old fillings, and bad breath. You don't even have to open your mouth."

With his suit's arms down again, Bryan could no longer see. He grabbed the armpits, kneeled on the suit's crotch, and pulled his head into the helmet. Through the tinted faceplate he could spy as Mr. Keen waved the dental device along his own jaw. It chimed as though the man had won bonus points in some video game.

"I, of course, have perfect teeth," he explained. "But holes—cavities, I should say—set off an alarm."

Spot regarded him with mistrust, her lips clamped, as he waved the tooth tester along both of her cheeks. Her pigtails stuck straight out like cow horns. Amazed, Bryan saw her eyes grow round, and she giggled.

"Don't worry," Mr. Keen advised. "That's our molar-magneto technology. You should see what it does to wigs and toupees."

Spot must have felt something else, though. She reached toward her dog collar, where tiny sparks jumped along its metal studs. Mr. Keen didn't notice, but the instant her fingers touched the collar, the Mouth Examiner rattled off a sharp *ack-ack-ack*.

"Aha! Fillings!" Mr. Keen shouted. "Easier that way for everyone." Just then, the noise warbled and stopped. The man cocked his head. "Hmm. Strange. I don't suppose you'd open wide and let me take a look?"

Spot curled her lip, growling.

"That's a start," he said cheerfully, crouching to study Spot's bared front teeth. "Ah, this may have caused the confusion. You have two sets of eye teeth. Both the baby and adult pairs, per—"

He reached one gloved finger toward her mouth. Spot snapped to bite. Mr. Keen jerked his hand back.

"Oh, dear, no insult intended," he assured her. "Believe me, I've seen teeth much stranger than yours. Or was that just your dentophobia showing?" At her unrepentant glare, he chuckled. "Well, I have been bitten all over the world; you would not be the first. You seem to have fillings in there somewhere, though. That's good enough for me. Go back to the guardhouse, if you like." He reached to fling open the door.

Spot dashed out and slammed the door shut behind her.

"Thank goodness," sighed Mr. Keen, following after her. "I'll get the boy next."

Bryan gulped.

"Get the drill ready," the man added over his shoulder to the suit. "If he really has no fillings, as he said, we'll have to install one—whether he needs it or not."

Bryan slipped his head back out of the helmet. Mr. Keen wouldn't find his seed stomper in the lobby. What then? Sweat tickled down his chest. *Right into my lunch*, he thought.

The sandwiches! He reached in and yanked out a strip of aluminum foil. With his other hand he found the end of the zipper again. In one swipe, he split the back of the suit and tumbled out. Silently begging the empty robot to stay put and not tattle on him, he scrambled to the blue doorway.

Mr. Keen scowled in the lobby.

"My turn?" Bryan asked. "I'm ready for my checkup! This is the place, right?"

Surprise flashed in Mr. Keen's face. "Why, yes,

very good. You must have been invisible there for a moment. Not learning new tricks, are you?" He eyed Bryan.

"I'm just not scared of the dentist like Spot."

As Mr. Keen waved him toward the dental chair, Bryan stuffed his foil into his mouth. He bit down and chewed fast. The scraping felt awful, like chomping electrified gum. Trying not to make a face, he hopped onto the chair. Mr. Keen explained his tooth tester, then waved it around Bryan's head.

The metallic lump in Bryan's molars tasted like pennies. He crossed his fingers, hoping the tooth tester would be fooled. He had no idea what he would do if it wasn't.

Ack-ack-ack—the familiar noise gave Bryan a hint of relief. The sound was awfully faint, though. Frowning, Mr. Keen held the tool to his ear.

"I thought you said you didn't have fillings?"

"Almost. I just got my first one." Bryan cranked his jaw wide for an instant to point at the metal jammed in his molars. He clicked his teeth tight again.

"Old-fashioned silver. Hmm." Mr. Keen pursed his lips. "Well, that'll do. Send in the next patient, will you?"

After shaking Bryan's hand, he turned to thrust

the tooth tester at the robot. "Here," he told it. "Check the battery in this."

Bryan slipped down from the chair. His trick had worked! To distract his boss from his wobbling knees, he asked, "Any seed stomping today? I didn't see the popcorn popper out back."

Mr. Keen shook his head. "Take the afternoon off. You'll have more than enough work tomorrow."

The robot followed Bryan to the door, the tooth tester clutched in fat fingers.

"Here! What's this?" Mr. Keen demanded. Bryan froze.

Mr. Keen grabbed the robot. "You've left your zipper undone!" Metal screeched as he yanked the zipper up. "An embarrassment, really." To Bryan's amazement and glee, the entire suit blushed pink. Mr. Keen dismissed it with a disgusted wave.

Gleaming white again in the lobby, the suit followed Bryan outside. Although he knew it was empty, the staring mask gave him the creeps. He edged out of reach. He wanted badly to scrape the foil from his teeth but was afraid the robot might somehow report him.

"Stop," Bryan commanded. He pointed. "Go over there." The robot ignored him.

A flush of worry warmed Bryan's skin. Why did

Mr. Keen want fillings in everyone's teeth? Maybe Acme could track you on radar that way. Even worse, some sinister remote control might send radio waves to your fillings and on to your brain. Bryan sucked in a sharp breath. If Tripper had fillings, and she probably did, that might explain her mice: Acme's mind control had already started.

No wonder a guy with false teeth couldn't get hired. Wait until Dad heard about Mr. Keen's dental work! He might not believe it without proof, though. Bryan eyed the robot trailing behind him. If he could get it to follow him home, Dad could take it apart and see what made it work.

Just then, the suit veered away. While he still had a chance, Bryan snatched the dental detector from the robot's gloved hand and took off through the gate.

15

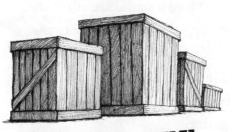

DO YOU SEE
WHAT I SEE?

Bryan stole a peek over his shoulder, but no Acme robot chased behind. Disappointed, he slowed. Still, the tooth tester bouncing in his pocket should help convince Dad.

As Bryan passed through the office, his feet stuttered to a halt. Small green bats flitted near the ceiling, then swooped at his head. They darted so quickly they were tough to count, but there were at least six or eight. He'd never seen any so small or so green, and he'd never seen any at all in the daytime.

He found his father giving Oscar a bath. "Dad! Did you know you've got bats in your office?"

The look on Dad's face made it clear this was news. Taking advantage of his surprise, Oscar leapt from the washtub and dashed off.

Grumbling, Dad followed Bryan and the dog's sudsy trail toward the office. Except for a faint whiff of flea shampoo, the air there was still.

"There were bats! Flitting all over!" Bryan flapped his arms. "Little green bats."

Dad drew a long breath, trying to hold his temper. "That was not the best timing for a joke," he growled. "Now help me catch Oscar before he—"

"Okay, but look at this first." Bryan pulled his stolen evidence from his pocket.

"A carrot?"

Bryan stared at the vegetable in his hand. Dad was right. It was the same shape as the tooth tester, but it was definitely a carrot. The tip held teeth marks, not a curly point or a light. He crammed his hand back into the pocket where the Anti-Cavity Mouth Examiner should have been. The Tater-Nugget fit snugly in the pocket's farthest corner. Otherwise, it was empty.

Bryan's mouth started talking without him. He told how Mr. Keen had checked Spot's teeth, and he waved the carrot by his own cheek to demonstrate. "Ack-ack-ack," he said, mimicking the noise he had heard.

Dad folded his arms and pulled his lips to one side. "He must have been teasing."

"No, he used it on me, too. But it wasn't a carrot. It was this electric device. I know it sounds weird, but it wasn't a carrot when I put it into my pocket!" Stumped, Bryan stared at it. The tool was like the flat Oscar—one thing going into his pocket, something else coming out. He scraped the foil from his teeth, in case even foil picked up Acme's mind control waves. The dental device still looked and felt like a carrot.

"That can't be good for your teeth," Dad chided.

"Mr. Keen said if I didn't have fillings, he'd make one whether I needed it or not."

"So he put aluminum foil on your teeth?" Finally Bryan's father sounded concerned.

"No! I did that to fool him!"

Dad rubbed his brow. He wasn't getting the right idea. Bryan hurried to explain.

"See, Spot had on her dog collar and that fooled it, I guess, or shorted it out, I couldn't really see because I was stuck in a robot, so he didn't drill her teeth, but I didn't *have* a dog collar and she ran out and I didn't have time to think of anything else because I had to unzip the robot fast, but my sandwiches were all squished in my shirt and that gave me the idea for the foil."

A moment passed while Bryan's words seemed to spread out and soak in, like water from an overflowed toilet. Dismayed, he reached into his shirt and pulled out what was left of his lunch. It looked like something that might grow in a swamp. But ripped foil and smashed sandwiches were the only firm proof of the morning's events he had left.

Dad wrinkled his nose and pitched the sandwiches into the trash. He asked carefully, "This all happened while you were planting popcorn?"

Bryan took a deep breath to slow his mouth. "No, no planting today. Today Mr. Keen was drilling teeth."

"And Mr. Keen would want to drill your teeth because . . . ?"

"I haven't figured that out yet. But I think he wants to control people's minds."

"Right. I think it's time for you to retire," Dad said. "Before you get fired, maybe. I guess you're too young for that kind of job, after all."

Bryan's heart sank. He hadn't told it right, and now his dad had it all wrong.

"It sounds to me like you're spending too much time with that girl, the one who pretends she's a dog," Dad continued. "One kid with delusions is enough for this town."

It hurt that his father thought he was nuts. It terrified Bryan as well, because a dad who thought his son had gone wacky might rethink the whole idea of being a dad. Maybe it sounded far-fetched, but his mother had changed her mind about being a wife and a mom, hadn't she? He couldn't go through that again; he would have no parents left.

Staring at the carrot, Bryan wished Tripper were there. She might be bossy, but she would believe him.

He whispered, "It's not a delusion."

"She really is a dog? Hoo-boy. You can turn in your resignation this afternoon."

"But—"

"No buts. Sorry, pal." Shaking his head, Dad turned to follow Oscar's drying tracks. "Let me find the darn dog, then I'll get you a fresh lunch."

Stunned, Bryan trailed behind. He didn't care about eating. Somehow his pocket had ruined the evidence he'd snatched, and he wouldn't have a chance to find more. Even worse, he'd just been demoted. He wanted his father to see him as a partner who could help pay the bills. Instead, Dad now saw him as a silly kid who hung out with crackpots, invented wild stories, and needed a keeper. Dad was probably thinking that sons were a pain in the neck, and Bryan couldn't risk any explanation that might backfire further. Nothing was working out as he wanted.

He slipped into the bathroom to think. Setting the carrot on the edge of the sink, he squished soap back and forth between wet hands and wondered. If he'd been able to lure an Acme robot home, would his father have been able to see it? Or was it all in Bryan's head, as Dad seemed to think? But Spot and Tripper had seen or heard plenty. He could share what he'd learned with either of them, but his chances of solving the mystery himself now were just about nil. He was Zilcher the Zero again.

A gurgle echoed under his feet. He turned off the faucet, but the noise didn't stop. *Splash!* Water sprinkled his shirt.

"Hey," Bryan said, spotting the source of the splash. A small plastic pop bottle bobbed in the toilet bowl. It must have shot backward through the pipes like a torpedo. Instead of explosives, this torpedo carried a twist of paper inside—a note in a bottle!

Bryan fished out the bottle and rinsed it in the sink in case it had touched anything gross. Then he twisted the cap off and drew the paper out.

One side warned, "Do not flush! Acme Inc. not responsible for plumbing damage caused by unauthorized use." On the other side, someone had jotted, "Big day tomorrow—please come to work at the first crack of dawn or no later than eight." Below that was added, "P.S. Don't eat the small item you took from the storeroom. We don't have many spares." It didn't need to be signed.

Bryan crushed the note in his fist. Despite the TaterNugget warning, Mr. Keen apparently did not know everything. Bryan would not be at work by eight or any other time. He stuffed the bottle, the note, and the stupid carrot in the clothes hamper. Dad could find them there later, for all he cared.

16

MIND MISCHIEF

I suppose I've been leaning on you too much," Dad mused.

"No, you haven't," Bryan said. He picked at the fresh lunch his father had made.

"Yes. It's fine to be pals, but I've got to remember my job as your dad. I can't expect you to look after yourself so much."

The words, which should have been reassuring, only reinforced Bryan's fears. A gravelly voice inside used to whisper that if he'd been more clever or needed less looking after, perhaps he'd still have a mom. Even now he sometimes felt that if he were anyone special, she would still want to see him. His father had denied it dozens of times, but that whisper would not go away.

Trying to shush it again, Bryan poked dents in his sandwich like the holes he'd poked in the dirt yesterday. Mr. Keen might be up to no good, but at least he didn't think Bryan needed a babysitter. The Acme president had trusted him to plant all by himself, and Bryan had worked the whole day without somebody watching. Mr. Keen had called it excellent work, too. What did Dad know?

Bryan squished the rest of his mangled sandwich into his napkin and slipped from his chair, his face downcast.

"Guess I better tell Mr. Keen I can't come back tomorrow."

Dad hesitated, then nodded. "Come straight home again, though. And stay close this afternoon, son. Tripper's bringing dinner at six."

Feeling like an ant under a steamroller, Bryan trudged back toward the factory. Frustration and dust swirled around him. He almost didn't notice when little Alison Merk, the bubble-blower, wiggled pudgy fingers at him from her doorstep. Seeing her, he realized he shouldn't be so obsessed with his own problems: Dad might have doomed all of South Wiggot by making him quit. Nearly everyone he knew had a filling or two, if not root canals or retainers or braces. Not counting toddlers like Alison and toothless geezers, Bryan might be the only person in town whose mind could not be controlled—the only one who could see the truth. His dad had no natural teeth to fill, but now he wouldn't believe anything Bryan said.

He looked askance at the post office as he passed it. The one adult who might listen to his mind control theory would be certain to take over and keep Bryan away from the action. If Tripper worried about pollution, mind control would send her ballistic.

Then Bryan remembered the Dog Girl. He still had an ally. Energized, he raced toward Spot's house.

He had just turned down her front walk when something attacked. White powder flew into his face. Sputtering, he brushed it off as fast as he could.

"Oops." Spot peeked from around a shrub. "It's just you."

With an exasperated grunt, he demanded, "What is that?" He sniffed. It smelled like Italian food.

Spot showed him a shaker of garlic salt. "For vampires! This was all I could find."

"*Vampires?*" Bryan's breath caught. Things were getting so weird, he was ready to believe anything.

"Vampires aren't real," he added. "But if you saw one, I'll bet I know why."

Raising a finger to her lips, Spot waved him into a shadow alongside her house. They sat against the wall in a sprinkling of garlic salt.

When she was satisfied they were safe, she whispered, "I sneaked onto my brother's computer at lunchtime. I looked up Acme on the Internet."

A pang of jealousy scorched Bryan. It seemed unfair that someone who pretended to be a dog had a computer at home when he was still saving for one. Stuck with handwritten notes in a pillowcase, he'd just lost his place as lead detective.

"So?" He tried not to sound cross.

Spot didn't notice. "You know where they came from? Bermuda. As in the Bermuda Triangle."

"No way!" Bryan had written a report last year on the Bermuda Triangle. Planes and ships vanished mysteriously there all the time.

"Yip," Spot confirmed. Her eyes glowed at his reaction. "Before that, Roswell, New Mexico—where the government guys found a crashed UFO. And dead aliens. They just won't admit it."

"Okay," Bryan said slowly. Mind control might be involved in both places. "But what's that got to do with vampires?"

Spot sprinkled more garlic. She whispered, "Acme's been *lots* of weird places. But you know where they started?" She hid her neck above her collar with both hands. "Transylvania, where Count Dracula's from. One bite and you join the Undead."

Bryan couldn't believe his ears. Spot's discovery cast new light on the Acme chief's interest in teeth: He may have been checking for fangs.

"And Mr. Keen even told me he's been bitten all over the world. By bloodsuckers, I bet that's what he meant."

Bryan squirmed. Part of him wanted to jump up, or hug Spot, or scream. The other part, the jealous part, insisted it couldn't be true. They'd seen Mr. Keen in the daytime, for starters. He supposed the man might be a vampire's assistant, hauling coffins and luring victims within easy reach, but daylight was not the only objection. Vampires had not likely put mail in his toaster or made Tripper see teabags instead of mice.

"That's just a story," he argued. "Lots of people must come from there. Besides vampires, I mean. Anyway," he added, frustration making him cranky, "you're practically a werewolf, Dog Girl. Should I be scared of you, too?"

Spot's face crumpled. She scrambled to her feet.

"I'm sorry," he said, wincing. "I take that back! Don't go!"

She ignored him. Her sneakers pounded around the corner and over the porch.

"Wait!" Desperate, Bryan jumped after her. "I've got a theory, too! I was inside one of the white suits! They're robots! I'll tell you what I—"

Wham! The door slammed. He'd chased one more person away.

Bryan slunk down the front walk and back to the road. He stared at the factory in the distance. With ideas about bloodsuckers and mind control crowding his head, he didn't want to go back after all—not by himself. And he'd never felt so alone.

17

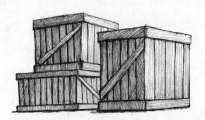

MESSED-UP
MESSAGES

As he stood near Spot's house, trying to decide what to do, something tickled Bryan's ear. A shadow passed over his head. He ducked, expecting a bloodthirsty bat. Instead, a blue balloon bobbed on the breeze. Its dangling string had brushed by him. More balloons floated beyond.

With a leap, he caught the nearest string and yanked. *POP!* Confetti showered onto his head. Right away Bryan spied the code: Each snippet of paper contained two or three typewritten letters. Together they must form some message!

He pinched up the bits before the breeze blew

them away. As his palm filled with crinkled paper, he remembered the other balloons and looked up. Bright dots glittered in the distance, already off to Alien Headquarters or Vampire Central or wherever they were bound.

Hoping he'd gotten enough, he trapped his coded confetti against his chest and headed back home. Who needed Spot? He'd show them all.

Once back in the station, he climbed onto his bed and raised it all the way to the top, where he could decode his confetti in private. First he uncrimped all the snippets of paper, laying them out in lines:

Ope	Mo	le
rat	uth	le
io	muf	ak
n	fl	ing
on	ing	w
sch	do	or
ed	ne.	se.
ule.	Ho	

He tried to arrange them like pieces from a word game. The capital letters and periods seemed like good clues. But after two hours, the best Bryan could come up with was "Open on schedule. Mole or rat waking mufiose. Hole doing fluthne." It didn't make much sense. The factory was indeed open, and moles and rats both made holes, but Bryan couldn't even find *mufiose* or *fluthne* in the dictionary.

Tripper's arrival interrupted his work. She acted

as though they'd never talked about Acme or mice. The adults blabbed all through dinner. Frustrated, Bryan strung macaroni on the tines of his fork. One minute he wanted to get Tripper alone and share his latest discoveries. The next he feared that would only make matters worse.

She noticed his silence. "You're not chowing down like usual." She paused, picking her words. "Feel okay? Bad day at work?"

Bryan grimaced. Was she asking veiled questions about their secret—or playing dumb?

"I told Bryan today that he had to quit his job," Dad explained.

"Oh." Tripper pressed her fork to her lips. "Something more interesting will come along," she added, encouragingly.

"You mean something less dangerous?" The sneer escaped before Bryan could stop it. "How about catching mice?"

Tripper paled.

"Hey, mister," Dad warned. "Watch your tone. I know you're disappointed, but that doesn't make it okay to be rude."

His gaze on the table, Bryan squeezed out an apology. Everyone knew he didn't mean it.

"Can I be excused now?" he added.

Dad exhaled hard. "I suppose. Take your plate. We'll talk more about this later."

Too crabby to worry about later, Bryan dumped his scraps into the dog's dish. Oscar ignored the macaroni, leaping instead at Bryan's shorts.

"What's with you?" Bryan wondered. Then he remembered the TaterNugget still in his pocket. He pulled it out. Barking, Oscar jumped for it. Bryan yanked his hand higher, then stuffed the nugget back into his pocket. The toilet-bottle warning aside, food that old couldn't be good, even for a dog.

"What is that?" Dad asked.

"Just a hunk of potato I picked up." He saw no point in mentioning where.

Tripper giggled. "Boy, that could make a mess in the wash!" She gave Bryan a lopsided grin. He scowled, sure she was trying to get him into even more trouble.

"Don't laugh," Dad told her. "I hope you'll be sharing our laundry one of these days."

Bryan froze. Tripper might move in?

"Whoa!" she demanded. "Richard Zilcher, did you just say what I *think* you just said?"

Dad's lips parted but no sound came out. A silent conversation flashed between the adults. Watching,

Bryan felt like he was hearing the last few ticks of a bomb.

He flinched when Tripper finally laughed.

"I'll pretend that did not sound like a marriage proposal," she said. "Your stinky socks may be alone awhile yet." She pushed back her chair and picked up their dishes. As she passed, she patted Bryan's shoulder. He cringed. He didn't want her to touch him. Still, it got his lungs going again.

The pocket potato forgotten, Dad jumped up, too. He dodged around his son to whisper to Tripper. Scared of what he might overhear, Bryan fled.

18

WEIRD SCIENCE— OR JUST WEIRD

Bryan dashed through the station. He shook his head to whisk away the chance that he might cry. The idea of Tripper's girly underwear swishing around in their wash was bizarre, but the two adults had been making faces at each other for well over a year. Bryan and his father had even talked once about Dad getting married again. They'd only been imagining then, but privately Bryan had already decided. His mom was not coming back, not for his dad and apparently not even for him. It had been months and months since her last note, jotted on one of those free motel postcards. Tripper helped fill the hole. He knew he could do worse for a stepmom.

But that opinion had been formed before any dispute over his job. Suddenly Tripper seemed to be meddling in Bryan's life, and worse, hijacking his dad.

He shoved out the door into the still evening. Taillights winked down the highway. Staring, Bryan rubbed the heels of his hands together until the skin burned. The heat matched what he felt in the pit of his stomach. He wondered how much money he needed to run away.

He scurried back into the office and straight to his money can. A choked exclamation left him. The metal was dented as if firecrackers had gone off inside, and the plastic lid had popped off and fallen nearby. Bryan's booby trap was a joke: Every silver coin had vanished, along with the bills. All that remained were the pieces of seven, like eyes glowing under the bed.

"Gone!" Bryan gasped. It was bad enough that he'd lost his job and along with it the inside chance to solve the only mystery South Wiggot had ever had. But his life savings, too?

Green flitted past his cheek. Bryan ducked and spun. A ten-dollar bill hovered like a butterfly near his shoulder. He snatched it. When he unfurled his fingers, the money rustled, then lay still. Bryan realized with a hiccup of disbelief that this was one of his bats.

He looked up. More money bats huddled in the gap between the light and the ceiling, where they must have been hidden all along. An origami master couldn't have made the bills look more like folded wings. He may have had pristine teeth, but something was messing with Bryan's head, that was clear— or with his money, at least.

Amazement and anger fought to work his tongue. The winner wanted to yell for his dad. Bryan clamped his teeth shut. His skeptical dad would be no help at this point.

"Get down here!" he hissed. He climbed onto Dad's desk and swiped at the fluttering bills. They swarmed down toward his head. Finally he trapped them all in his hands like falling leaves. Gripping them tightly, he scooped the warped can under one arm and marched out.

Mr. Keen responded promptly when Bryan pounded on Acme's office door.

"Here so soon? I didn't hear dawn crack." Mr. Keen cupped his long fingers near his ear. "In fact, it still sounds like today. So today can't be yest—"

"Cut the tricks! I know something weird is going

on, but I won't let you rob me! Give me my money back!" Bryan thrust his battered can forward.

Mr. Keen's eyebrows practically shot into orbit. "I'm afraid I don't have it." He inspected the can. "Ah. You kept your money in here?"

"Until it escaped!" He didn't care how goofy it sounded. "These were flying around the room." He waved the bills trapped in his fist. Several squirmed loose to flap onto Mr. Keen's shoulders.

The man rolled his eyes. "I'm sorry, truly. Money is fond of me. I think it's my hair gel. That's why I suggested pieces of seven—they're too heavy to fly."

"Quarters can't fly, but all my change is gone, too!" Seeing Mr. Keen hold back a smile, Bryan added, "It's not funny. It's not fair. And it's not my imagination!"

"No, indeed." Mr. Keen drummed his fingers on the can. "I won't try to explain. You'd better come see for yourself."

"See what?" Bryan's eyes narrowed. He'd run to the factory without much idea of what to expect. Now a nervous jolt hit him; he wasn't sure about going inside.

Mr. Keen simply led him around to the field. Silver insects flitted above the dandelions. It took Bryan only a second to see that the silver flashes weren't wings. They were nickels and quarters and dimes, whirring like metal bees.

"It's the pieces of seven, I'm afraid," said Mr. Keen. "They get ordinary money riled up. First it multiplies. Then, if it's not in the proper container, it just can't sit still."

Bryan stared. "No way. Money isn't alive! It's some kind of trick."

"Who said anything about it being alive?" Mr. Keen waved his hands. "It's driven by excited molecules, quivering quarks, and lionized ions. Or is it ionized lions? I forget. Never mind. How much science have you studied in school?"

"It's not my best subject," Bryan admitted.

"I suspected as much. Technology and tricks look much alike if you don't know an electron from an elephant and you can't fit a nanobot into your noodle."

"I guess so." Bryan sighed, his head aching. He eyed Mr. Keen. "But how do I get my money back?"

The man snatched a passing coin from the air. "It's not hard to catch," he said, dropping the dime into Bryan's palm. "Keeping it caught is the tricky part. Hmm." He tapped his nose. "I know—when we harvest tomorrow, we'll get the coins, too. You can have them all back then, plus interest. In the meantime, how can Acme make it up to you? You've been an excellent seed stomper, despite all the problems we've caused you. How can I make amends?"

Bryan watched the silver glinting in the late sun and reminded himself that Mr. Keen was probably dangerous. He treated Bryan right, though. He talked to him like an adult and believed what Bryan said. What would happen if the Acme chief found out that a kid was onto some of his secrets?

"There must be something you want," Mr. Keen prompted. "Try me."

"Okay, wise guy," Bryan said, trying to sound tough. "Spill the beans. What are you doing here, really? Why do you care about teeth? What's with the white robots? And what's in there behind the red door?" He almost added, "Last but not least, what kind of Trouble has a capital *T*?" He decided to hang on to that secret.

He expected a lot of big words or some lame excuse. Instead, Mr. Keen flashed his teeth. They reminded Bryan more of an angry dog than a grin.

"I thought you'd never ask."

19

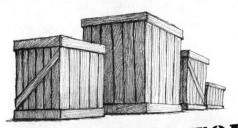

A TANTALIZING TOUR (AND SOME TRUTH)

The freshly painted lobby was deserted. The dental patients all had gone home. Mr. Keen ushered his seed stomper through the lobby's third door—the red one. *Blood red*, Bryan thought with a gulp. He held his breath.

Their footsteps echoed in the cleanest, brightest room Bryan had ever seen. It made a doctor's office look cluttered and unsanitary. Fresh white paint sparkled from floor to ceiling, dazzling his eyes. He started breathing again.

The room wasn't as empty as it first appeared. A glass chute dropped from a hatch in the ceiling and fell in big loop-de-loops like a waterpark slide, except that the landing would hurt: The chute ended in a tangle of glass funnels and pipes right in the center of the room. It rather resembled the chemistry supply shelf at school.

"Wow." As Bryan approached the crystal contraption, he noticed a number of odd parts. A yellow balloon bulged at the end of one tube. At the opposite end, goldfish swam in what looked like a gumball machine. Air bubbles rose from the gumballs. Not far away, copper wires linked a short row of familiar green lumps.

"Are those . . . Brussels sprouts?" Bryan asked doubtfully, pointing.

"If you're in a vegetable frame of mind, I suppose," Mr. Keen replied. "Acme is not. Everything here is an important part of our production and packing line."

"What's it make?"

"Acme Ink! I thought that was clear." Mr. Keen reached into the glassworks and pulled out a squat bottle with what looked like spit bubbles inside. With a start, Bryan recognized the bottle's shape. His ears just couldn't tell a *C* from a *K*.

"I get it—ink. But it's dried up."

"Invisible," Mr. Keen corrected. "What you see isn't the ink. We add those air bubbles to distinguish the empty bottles from the full ones."

Doubt sprouted in Bryan's mind. "I thought invisible ink was just lemon juice."

"Pshh. Cheap imitation. You can see lemon juice. The real thing uses microscopic elements. Awfully Clever Microscopic Elements, that is. See?"

"Not really." Invisibility could be real, though, Bryan had to admit. Some of the invisible things on your skin were pretty creepy, if you looked at them with a microscope.

"Top secret, of course," Mr. Keen added. He

winked. "Most of our customers have no names, just initials: CIA, NSA, MIB, MOM. But somebody has to sell them supplies. And there's only so much our robots can do, even if they are quite advanced." He stuck out his arms and stiffened his knees.

Recognizing the zombie imitation, Bryan shuddered. He ventured, "But they don't seem to have any motors or gears." He knew for certain they didn't, but he didn't want to admit he'd been inside one.

"I told you they were advanced. They use low-frequency, digital motion injectors."

Bryan gave Mr. Keen a sideways look. "I thought it might be mind control."

The man never flinched. "They don't have any minds to control. They just do what they're programmed to do, like the robots that put together new cars."

No signs of a fib appeared in Mr. Keen's face. Bryan pressed, "So they're not suits to protect against radiation or poisons?"

"I've told them and told them," Mr. Keen muttered, shaking his head. "No indeed. But they have to look like *something,* you know. We've tried more cuddly robots. One had fake fur. Small children kept dragging it off. People avoid this model, and that's just as well."

Bryan walked alongside the glass piping. "Okay, but once the ink's made, where does the factory's pollution go?"

Mr. Keen arched an eyebrow. "Who said there was any? Invisible ink is one hundred percent natural. There's no pollution when you squeeze apples into apple juice, is there? Invisible ink's just the same." He lifted a nozzle and waved it. "There's a bit of pulp left, but we find a good use for that, too. No waste at all."

Thinking of the dandelion army out back, Bryan started to ask what got squeezed, but was struck by a better idea. A surprise question might throw the man off.

"Then why do you make sure there are fillings in everyone's teeth?"

The olive eyes narrowed. Bryan's heart tripped. Was that guilt? But Mr. Keen didn't try to erase the look from his face. Instead, he plopped his hands on his knees. He whispered, "Can I trust you with an Acme trade secret?"

The biggest blabbermouth in the county would have nodded. Bryan certainly did.

"Do you know how hard it is to make invisible products?" Mr. Keen asked. "Think of spills, robbery, accidents—how would you know?"

"I see what you mean. But what's that got to do with teeth?"

"Imagine drowning in a flood of invisible ink." Mr. Keen pinched his nose. Knees knocking, elbows flapping, he pretended to drown. He looked more like a grasshopper doing jumping jacks, but Bryan's giggle stuck in his throat.

"We can't have distraction around invisible ink," the man gasped. "Toothaches can be terribly distracting. What if a distracted employee broke a pipe or forgot to turn off a valve? Catastrophe! So cavities must be fixed at all cost."

"What about false teeth?" Bryan asked, remembering his dad.

"Even worse!" Mr. Keen drew back one eyelid so that his eye bulged like a golf ball. "A glass eye once popped out at just the wrong time! Ruined a whole batch! Not to mention the eye. Since then our policy has been strict: No false eyes, teeth, or fingernails, no wigs or toupees. No false ears or elbows either. No false parts allowed at all."

This explanation sounded pretty convincing— and much more likely than mind control waves. Disappointed, Bryan pulled at his lips. He was forgetting something. All of Mr. Keen's answers seemed to work in reverse, sucking information out of his head.

Mr. Keen tapped a glass tube. "Production is not up to speed yet, of course," he said. Folding his hands, the Acme chief tipped his head in a gracious salute. "For that we need you."

Bryan blushed, but he stood taller, too. Acme needed *him* to get anything done. Boy, that felt good.

"Any more questions?" Mr. Keen asked.

Bryan examined the ink bottle in his hand. A top-secret product—was that what the locals didn't suspect? All those government acronyms on the customer list probably would cause trouble if their secret got out. But Trouble? And surely a company with invisible ink and the technology to make quarters fly didn't need to send notes on dogs and inside balloons. Where would such messages go, and to whom? Bryan was dying to ask, but he wasn't sure he should give away all he knew.

When he glanced up, Mr. Keen was marching back toward the red door. Bryan slipped the bottle into his pocket, hoping to test it later. He trotted to catch up.

"Step lively, then! Morning will be here any minute. And your misbehaving money will be back in your hands before you go home tomorrow." The man skidded to a halt. "By the way, you haven't got a hole in your pocket, have you?"

Bryan's face burned. Reluctantly, he drew the ink bottle back out. "No. But I still have this."

Mr. Keen pursed his lips. "Oh, I'd better take that. How about your socks? Any holes there?"

Bryan shook his head. He hated it when a toe poked through a frayed spot. The toe always felt like it was choking.

"May I see, please? Sock holes can be sly."

Bryan kicked off his sneakers. One sock's heel was thin. Otherwise they were quite snug.

"Never mind. The hole I want will turn up."

Abruptly recalling the *Hole* in his confetti message, Bryan gasped. "What hole?"

Mr. Keen only whirled and disappeared through the red doorway.

20

ON THE HUNT
FOR A HOLE

Wait!" Bryan grabbed his shoes and scurried after Mr. Keen. The red door clunked shut behind him, leaving him surrounded by darkness and an unpleasant smell. Then the roof swung open to let in golden light. Instead of the lobby, Bryan found himself in a metal Dumpster. Confused and dizzy, he swayed and clutched his shoes to his chest.

Mr. Keen's face appeared overhead. He helped Bryan climb out. Safe on the ground, Bryan recognized the Dumpster. It was the blue one behind the factory. Beyond the weedy field, a cherry sliver on the horizon marked the setting sun.

"How'd we get back here?"

"Back door, naturally. You must have gotten turned around."

More like inside out, Bryan thought. He remembered Mr. Keen's words a moment before. "What did you mean back there about a hole?" he asked. "A hole in what?"

Mr. Keen smiled slyly as though he were about to give away some juicy secret. Abruptly he ground his palms together. "Come to work first thing! Maybe you'll see!"

Bryan groaned. "I can't. My dad told me I have to quit."

For an instant, he would have sworn that a bolt of white steam shot from each of the man's oversized ears. The vapor vanished as fast. Mr. Keen launched a flurry of questions. "Have we worked you too hard? Put you in danger? Paid you unfairly?"

"What you pay me keeps flying away!" Bryan protested.

"Besides that. That's easy to fix. What's the *real* reason?" Mr. Keen leaned knowingly toward him.

Bryan's mouth fumbled. He couldn't admit that he'd stolen the tooth tester, even if it did turn out to be a carrot. "I try to tell my dad about my job," he said, "and he thinks I'm making things up. He thinks it's Spot's fault."

Mr. Keen put his chin in his palm and drummed his fingers on his cheekbone. "Put on your shoes," he said finally, "and leave it to me."

Bryan stuffed his feet back into his sneakers. When he looked up, he stood there alone.

He glanced uneasily into the building's vast shadows. The dandelions had folded shut for the night, and his coins must have settled down or flown off. Now light leaked fast from the sky. Nothing he'd seen inside had scared him, but Spot's theories and his own still had him spooked. Bryan stifled a shiver.

Before he left, though, he tried to figure out how the Dumpster led into the factory. He skipped pebbles underneath from one side to the other and he wiggled into the gap between the metal and the factory's cool, concrete wall. He couldn't see where they connected. He poked his finger into pockmarks in the concrete. None triggered a trap door. He dared himself to climb back into the Dumpster to check inside, but in the looming dark, he chickened out.

Back home, Bryan found the gas station empty except for the dog. Dad was probably somewhere with Tripper. That notion made Bryan's chest hurt.

Trying to ignore the ache, he cuddled Oscar briefly, then retreated to his bed to work a bit more on the code.

Once he'd pulled the snippets out of his pillow-case, he realized that some letters might be invisible. As far as he could tell, though, the message did not mention ink. The only *K* was attached to an *A*.

Bryan whistled. He sorted out letters for *leaking,* which might go with *Hole.* Mr. Keen had asked about a hole in his pockets or socks and then said "It'll turn up" as if it might show up anywhere. What could leak from such a hole? Certainly not invisible ink.

Musing, Bryan picked up the snippet that read *rat.* Tripper had mice. Double agents, like tattletales, were sometimes called rats. A small rat might chew holes in your teabags or socks, but tea leaks or toe leaks could hardly cause the end of the world. A big rat, on the other hand—a giant, alien, vampire rat— might chew a black hole through outer space and arrive through the Bermuda Triangle. A leaking hole like that could really spell Trouble. And wasn't that the sound of teeth gnawing on the walls even now?

Bryan jerked. He'd been dreaming. Dawn was sneaking into the station. He shook his head, sending bits of confetti tumbling from his hair. More clung to his cheek. He'd fallen asleep on the code. His father normally didn't let him sleep with his bed up near the ceiling, in case he rolled off. But Dad had not awakened him last night when he'd finally come home.

The gnawing sound from Bryan's dream had followed him back into reality, too. For a second he thought his belly might be to blame, but the growling didn't come from inside. He peered over the edge of his bed toward his father's below. He could see two sock-clad feet at the end of a long, Dad-shaped lump. Dad's head was buried somewhere under his pillow, but his muffled snores buzzed through the stuffing.

Bryan hid away his cryptic confetti and notes, planning what to do once he got out of bed. What if he just happened by Acme on his way somewhere else? He could visit Spot in the guardhouse, for instance, or sell LemonMoo by the gate. He recalled exactly what Dad had said yesterday. His job had been nixed, but the factory had not been forbidden— not in so many words.

The snores never paused as Bryan lowered his bed to the floor. He pulled on a clean T-shirt, not bothering to change the shorts he'd slept in. Grabbing two bananas for breakfast, he tiptoed outside. He was flirting with being grounded, but he had to take the chance. Mr. Keen had hinted that something big might happen today. If Bryan didn't keep an eye on the factory, at least from a distance, who knew what he might miss?

21

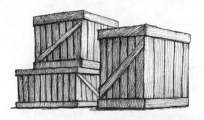

THE POOF-PICKER PIPE

Left hand here, right hand there. Lips in the middle. Paying attention?"

"Yes, sir. Lips in the middle." Bryan pulled his gaze back to Mr. Keen. It was hard not to keep looking over his shoulder. The two stood in the field behind the factory, and Bryan half expected his dad to arrive and drag him away.

"Then point the nozzle and puff." Mr. Keen thrust the white bag into Bryan's arms. It felt like a pillow with plumbing attached. A mouthpiece poked from the top. A trumpet horn dangled down from the middle, skimming the ground like a weed whacker. At first

Bryan had mistaken the contraption for a strange Scottish bagpipe. Then he realized he'd seen one before, in the storage room with Spot. The back of this bag hooked to a vacuum hose as thick as his leg, and yards of that hose stretched toward the factory roof. He suspected it ended at the glass chute in the ceiling he'd seen yesterday.

"Only puff, never slurp," Mr. Keen added. "Think tuba, not straw."

"Like this?" Bryan aimed the horn-shaped nozzle toward Mr. Keen's shoelace and blew into the mouthpiece. The bag screeched like old bedsprings. Instead of blowing air on the shoe, the nozzle sucked, lifting the man's whole foot into the air. As the sound faded, Mr. Keen stomped his shoe back into place.

"Bravo! No need to blow hard, though. We don't want you light-headed. Pretend you're blowing out a small birthday candle. Just one."

Bryan already felt light-headed, though it could have been from trying to decode confetti all night. Or it could have been guilt. He shoved the feeling away.

"Couldn't we just use a regular vacuum? We've got a—"

"Fifty years of research have gone into the Acme Poof-Picker Pipe," Mr. Keen informed him coolly. "It magnifies your puff ninety-three times, kills bad germs, reverses the polarity, and can outsuck three tons of quicksand. Can your Hoover do that?"

Bryan shook his head.

"I thought not." Mr. Keen squinted at the sun. It rested low in the sky, gathering strength before firing down hot summer rays. "It won't be long now. Get ready, get set—"

WHOOMPF! Startled, Bryan spun. The folded dandelion buds, so golden yesterday, had burst awake. A sea of round, cottony seed heads bobbed before him.

"Go!" cried Mr. Keen. Bryan aimed the nozzle at the nearest poof and gave a small puff. The fluffy seeds whisked into the pipe and shot through the fat hose to the roof.

"Marvelous! Keep at it! We'll be done in no time!"

Soon Bryan could scoop up dozens of puffballs at once. Mr. Keen had warned him not to let a single seed float away, lest the neighbors complain. Not one escaped.

As the sun warmed the field, Bryan spotted his coins. They'd been hiding under dandelion leaves, but now the silver rose to wink among the puffballs. At his boss's urging, he aimed the nozzle at the coins.

The Poof-Picker sucked them up with a clatter. He could feel them bounce through the bag and into the hose.

"I'll go make sure your coins are properly sorted," Mr. Keen said.

Once he was alone, Bryan searched the horizon every few minutes. He'd arrived at the factory planning only to talk to Spot. But the guardhouse had been empty. Maybe she'd been too scared of vampires.

He'd been peeking into the guardhouse window when he felt a tap on his shoulder. Bryan had cringed, prepared to be grounded, but the tap had not come from his father.

"Congratulations," Mr. Keen had said, standing there with the pipebag tucked under one arm. "You're hired."

"Huh?"

"We need a poof piper. You come highly recommended."

Bryan's lips twisted. Mr. Keen was suggesting a trick that Dad would call bending the rules. Bryan might be grounded even longer for that.

"We had a very good seed stomper," the Acme president continued, "but he quit. Leaving a *hole*."

Bryan gulped at the word choice. Mr. Keen's

sparkling eyes promised excitement. Bryan blew out a frustrated breath. "I wish I could, but my dad—"

"Oh, I've made all the necessary arrangements." Mr. Keen dumped his pipebag into Bryan's arms.

"You talked to my dad?"

"All parental objections have vanished." Mr. Keen winked. "Just in time, too. Come along!"

Bryan had followed, uncertain. He'd argued with himself the whole way, but he wanted to believe Mr. Keen. That's why he stood behind the factory now, huffing and puffing. Every breath felt like it might be his last before the yelling began.

As time passed, though, and no angry father appeared, Bryan began to relax. The pipebag screeched, the sun heated the top of his head, and his thoughts returned to holes and the Trouble they might cause if they leaked. He ran through every kind of hole he could think of: holes to China and holes in Swiss cheese, Alice's rabbit hole and the holes dug by that kid Stanley Yelnats. The ocean might leak out through the hole in the bottom of the sea, and radiation from the sun could leak in through the ozone hole in the sky.

Bryan pondered until he felt he had a hole in his head. Unless something could leak out of that, he couldn't see what any holes had to do with South Wiggot or invisible ink.

Suddenly it hit him: Cavities were holes, too—in your teeth! Bryan gasped. Then he choked, coughing. Gasping too close to the mouthpiece had worked the Poof-Picker in reverse. Mr. Keen had warned about that. From the tickle in his throat now, Bryan figured he must have sucked one or two tiny seeds right inside.

He cleared his throat and then spit. Fuzz still stuck in his throat, along with a faint taste of licorice. So he swallowed hard, twice. Gulping weed seeds was less disgusting than the gnats he sometimes caught while riding his bike. Swallowing fixed the tickle, anyway. Careful to only blow outward, Bryan got back to work.

Meanwhile, he puzzled. Had Mr. Keen been looking for cavities because those were holes, too? Or was Spot right, and the real threat came from vampire teeth making holes in somebody's neck? The tangle of riddles made Bryan's throat hurt.

By quitting time, the field was bare. He gratefully dropped the pipebag and coiled the big hose near the rear of the factory. The Dumpster yawned open today, empty paint cans piled inside. As he stretched his tired arms, he noticed one last weed seed caught on his sleeve. It seemed a shame not to wish on just one of those billions of seeds, so he plucked the stray free, held it high, and gave the day's final puff. It sailed into the blue.

"I wish . . . I wish I knew what kind of hole—"

WAAA-WAAA-WAAA! Sirens split the air. Bryan whirled. Mr. Keen slid down the hose from the roof like a firefighter slipping down a pole to a fire.

"What's the emergency? Aha." Mr. Keen snatched something out of the air. The sirens quit. "You missed one." The spidery fingers pinched the lone wishing seed Bryan had set free.

There goes that wish, Bryan thought. Aloud he said, "Whoops. Sorry." Luckily, Mr. Keen couldn't see the other mistake sucked down Bryan's gullet.

"It's forgiven. You've done so well overall." Mr. Keen tucked the fluff into his pocket. "Just don't let it happen again."

"How could it? There isn't a single one left."

The man's eyes gleamed. "We'll have more by Monday. In the meantime—" He snapped his fingers. A bankbook appeared there. The trick made Bryan's spine tingle.

"When I was your age, I dabbled in magic," Mr. Keen explained.

Bryan tried to picture his boss as a kid. The idea gave him the willies.

"All illusion, of course." Mr. Keen dropped the book into Bryan's hand. "This is quite real."

Bryan checked inside. Three hundred dollars had been deposited in his name.

"Wow, thanks," he breathed. His can couldn't have held half that amount.

"I took your coins to the bank," Mr. Keen explained. "Plus your wages today. I can promise that anything you withdraw will behave. A night in the vault always does it.

"Keep that in a pocket or desk, though," he added. "Not in a can. And certainly not up your sleeve. You'd be surprised by the things that can happen in a sleeve."

Bryan nodded. He shuffled his feet, then licked his lips.

"Something else?" Mr. Keen asked. "It's Friday. Don't you want to go home?"

Bryan looked both ways, then whispered, "Did that hole you mentioned turn up today?"

"Turn up?" The man shrugged. "Not that I noticed. But speaking of turnips, you owe me a carrot." Bryan winced at the mention of his theft, but Mr. Keen clapped him on the back. "And a Lemon-Moo, too, don't forget. All I've gotten so far is a can full of dents. Don't think I'm not keeping track."

"I'll run and get 'em now," Bryan offered, his face red.

"No. I have work to do yet. Messages I need to send." Was that a wink? "So *adios*," Mr. Keen finished. "*Au revoir*. Scram."

Bryan headed for the gate, keeping an eye out for stray dogs and balloons. He was tantalized by the feeling that Mr. Keen was leading him toward answers to all the riddles. Either that or the Acme president was teasing him while committing more sinister deeds out of sight.

22

A LUMP IN
THE THROAT

A flash caught Bryan's eye. Something twinkled in an apple tree not far away.

He glanced back at the factory. Was Mr. Keen sending Morse code to the tree? Nothing blinked from the building. The tree winked again, though.

His eyes on the gnarled tree, Bryan walked until a mound of briars hid him from view of the factory. Then he darted into the meadow and crept through the tall grass like a lion stalking a zebra.

His throat tickled. Afraid a cough would give him away, he choked it back, hurried beneath the tree's outstretched limbs, and looked up.

"Eeeee!"

Bryan lurched back, sure he'd tripped some alarm. Then he noticed that the tree had a leg capped by a sneaker, and he recognized the screech.

"Spot! What are you doing up there? Who are you signaling?"

A green apple zinged past Bryan's head. Dodging, he hoisted himself onto a branch of his own.

Growling, Spot turned her back and raised binoculars toward the factory. Sunlight glanced off the lenses—the mysterious flash. Bryan tried to swallow his disappointment.

He could hardly swallow at all. The lump in his throat felt as big as a pillow. When he finally let himself cough, feathers burst from his mouth.

"You're disgusting." Her nose wrinkled, Spot peered at him through the leaves.

"I didn't do it," Bryan protested, staring. Feathers could not possibly have been down his gullet. "They must have been stuck on this branch. I just knocked them loose." As the feathers drifted away, his throat began tickling again.

Eager to think of anything else, he asked, "What have you seen with those binoculars?"

Spot ignored him. A forlorn breeze hissed through the tree. Fidgeting on the scaly bark, Bryan agonized. He could just jump down and go home, but Dad and Tripper seemed to be plotting against him. He missed having someone to share secrets with. And he had to admit that Spot had never done anything but try to help him.

"I don't know what you're looking for," he said, "but I can tell you some things that might help." He began with the robot and went on to the carrot confusion and the money can mayhem. He only paused twice to clear his throat, which kept clogging. By the time he got to his pipebag duties that day, Spot had given up pretending that she wasn't listening and had slipped one branch closer.

"I saw you," she said, gripping her field glasses.

"Is that why you keep coughing? The wish seeds you sucked up?"

"I don't know. I thought I swallowed 'em, but can you see anything back there?" He yawned wide, then added, "Something flutters when I breathe." Indeed, he felt as if the butterflies that sometimes flopped in his stomach had migrated north to his neck.

Spot looked away. "I shared my garlic with you, and you were mean to me."

Bryan's yawn collapsed. "I'm sorry about that werewolf crack, really. Just jealous, I guess. I won't make fun of you ever again."

Spot tugged at her dog collar as if she, too, felt choked. His attention drawn to her neck, Bryan recalled how worried she'd been about Transylvania.

"Unless Acme turns you into a vampire," he added, trying to joke. "I might make fun of you then, if I don't have a wooden stake handy. You won't care once you're a bat."

Spot giggled. "I might be a bat-hound instead. I could say I got bit by Dracula's dog!"

Relieved by her reaction, Bryan echoed her laugh. "But instead of Spot we'd have to call you Fang," he pointed out, in an eruption of stressed-out silliness. "I'd have a friend who joined the Undead *and* the Undog!"

Spot sobered. "Are we friends?"

"Aren't we?" Chuckles still bubbled inside him.

"No matter what?"

His grin waning, Bryan imagined the worst possible test—the school bus. Zilcher the Zero standing up for his weird friend, the Dog Girl. Compared to the trials he'd been having at home, that didn't sound so bad.

"I promise," he said. "No matter wha-k-k-k." The last word strangled in his throat.

Hearing it, she raised the binoculars. "Open up." Her oversized eyes blinked at him through the lenses. Bryan obeyed.

"Something *is* stuck there," she reported.

"Let me see." Remembering how well they'd mirrored the sun, Bryan took the binoculars and caught his reflection in one lens. He tipped his head sideways, mouth gaping. The thing in his throat looked like some hairy insect, not a damp dandelion seed.

"Hck-k-k-k," he gargled, trying to dislodge it. It wobbled. He tried again, harder. A gray blob shot out, fluttering near the end of his nose. For a horrible instant Bryan thought he'd gargled loose one of his tonsils.

"A moth!" Spot cried. She cupped her hands to

catch it and peeked in through her fingers. "You had a moth in your mouth. Gross," she added.

"I couldn't!" he argued. "I didn't! I . . ." They'd both seen it happen. Spot held the proof. There *were* butterflies in him! As he finished that thought, the tickle returned.

"There's still something there, though," he moaned. His heart sped up. He slipped from the tree. "I'd better go home. Maybe I just need a drink." Bryan didn't believe it, but it made him feel more normal.

"I'm coming, too." Spot bounced down beside him. "I want to see what comes out of you next."

23

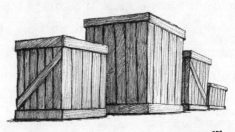

ZOMBIE PANTS

They had just reached the road when Bryan sneezed. He wasn't completely surprised to sneeze out a cascade of soap bubbles. It looked like he'd swallowed the bubble wand from his pillowcase file. Spot recoiled as bubbles popped near her head.

"A leaking hole," she mused. "It looks to me like things are leaking out of *you*. And your mouth is a kind of a hole—in your head."

"Very funny. It's that seed."

"I'm not joking," Spot said. "Maybe stuff really is leaking out of you, like bad dreams coming to life. Maybe that's what Mr. Keen meant by Trouble."

"I've never had dreams this crazy. Besides, before today none of the weird stuff I've seen came out of me." Bryan pulled on his lip. There *was* some link between his mind and the stuff now popping out of his throat, though. His brain gave him pictures of what the tickle felt like, then the results of a cough or a sneeze matched, more or less. Right now the feeling was scratchy, like a matchstick scraping a rock. Wait! Erase that! Too late. Bryan sneezed out a shower of red and blue sparks.

"Something's wrong with you, that's for sure," Spot said as the fireworks faded.

"Mr. Keen's hole is not in my head!" Reconsidering, Bryan added, "Not in my teeth, anyhow. No cavities, that is."

"Me neither. I brush extra good because I *hate* the dentist and I *never* want to get drilled. But so what?"

Bryan stared at her. "Everyone heard the explosions that first day, in the church. My dad heard the train. And Tripper could hear the mouse teabags. She just couldn't see 'em. Only I could. Maybe that's why."

Spot twisted one pigtail. "They say some people hear the radio on their braces. The wires turn into antennas. But we don't have wires."

"Maybe it's the opposite," Bryan replied, catching the tail of an idea. "Maybe fillings drown out the radio, like the blender drowning out the TV. Or like iron can goof up a compass." He smirked. "Mr. Keen told me they didn't want anyone distracted by a toothache. But maybe if you have fillings, you can't tune into the Acme Weirdness Channel—so you don't notice flat dogs!"

"Or winking waffles?" Spot shuddered at some memory.

"Or mice in your tea box," Bryan continued. Spot's question sank in. "Or wacky waffles, sure. You might hear things, but you can't see 'em at all! And folks with false teeth can't get fillings, so Mr. Keen doesn't want 'em around." He started to trot. He could test his theory with his next cough or sneeze. If he was right, Dad would see the same things he and Spot saw. Tripper wouldn't.

The station's office door creaked as they entered. Oscar peered out from under a chair and whined.

Alarmed by that unusual greeting, Bryan hurried through to the bay and hollered, "Dad! Are you home?"

"What a cool place to live," Spot murmured. "Can I spend the night sometime?"

Bryan blinked. He pulled a lopsided grin. Nobody had ever asked that before.

"I might let you," he said, the words tasting hotter than usual. A burning in the back of his throat hinted that something was ready to fly. He tried thinking of something slippery and cool, like his favorite ice cream—

Whoosh! Fire roared from his lips. It vanished as fast. It didn't hurt, and neither his shirt nor his eyebrows ignited. Spot still screamed.

"Cherry Bomb Blast," he explained. Vanilla might have been wiser.

"You'd better do something quick!" she said. "It's getting dangerous!"

Bryan hurried to the faucet, cranked it on, and slurped. The cool water felt nice in his throat, but it almost wouldn't go down. The lump there seemed to be growing. Where the heck was Dad, anyway?

Stay calm, he told himself. During the jog from the factory, Bryan had come up with a plan.

"The Shop-Vac," he told Spot. "That should suck it out."

They hurried to a heavy-duty vacuum stashed in one corner. Spot plugged it in while Bryan wrapped his lips around the nozzle.

She flipped the switch. Its motor whining, the vacuum sucked the breath clean out of Bryan's lungs.

His cheeks hollowed, and he felt as if his tongue and his teeth might be whisked out of him, too. Spot watched, her eyes round.

Skitter-klunk! Something clattered down through the hose. Bryan yanked the nozzle away and gasped in fresh air. His tongue checked his teeth. They were all still in place.

"Did you get it?" Spot switched off the vacuum. The motor died, but the rattle continued. The canister jumped, shaken by something upset trapped inside.

Spot backed away, her hands clutched to her throat. Bryan stood frozen, eyes bulging. He wanted to peek into the vacuum, but the thing inside might bite—or jump back down his throat! It was like living in a horror movie. His legs trembled and his mouth was too dry to swallow. But there was that crazy tickle again . . . the wishing seed was still there!

"Dad!" Since there was no sign of his father inside, Bryan dashed out back.

There he was! His father's legs, clad in jeans, stretched from beneath the tow truck. Dad tinkered with that truck all the time. He didn't usually work with his boots off, but the day had been hot. Maybe that's why only his socks poked from the cuffs of his jeans.

Bryan ran to the truck, trying not to pant. If he

inhaled the fluff deeper into his chest, the seed and the things it was hatching might never get out.

With Spot lagging behind, he stopped near Dad's socks. Would his father shout when he learned where the problem had started? Bryan's throat clenched. He didn't have any choice.

"Hey, Dad, there's something wrong with my throat." Shaky, he tapped his dad's foot.

A wrench fell with a bang to the cement. The little cart under Dad's legs skated out. Bryan saw his dad's knees, his front pockets, his belt—

"AAAAHHH! Daaaaad!" After the belt came a blank spot. Bryan leapt away. His dad's socks and pants—all that lay on the cart—bent at the knees and got up to walk off. By themselves! Bryan caught a

glimpse into the waist of his dad's jeans. They held nothing but air. If Dad were still somehow inside them, he had become utterly invisible.

Bryan stumbled back, falling hard on his tailbone. He heard a squeal that might have been Spot, but his ears and his head felt a long, woozy way from his body. He rolled over and buried his face in his arms, waiting for the zombie pants to attack.

24

VANISHING SPOT

The zombie pants did not come after Bryan. For all he knew, they'd wrapped their empty legs around Spot and dragged her off. For a moment he did nothing but gasp, eyes scrunched tight. Then his brain started again. He remembered Mr. Keen saying, "Parental objections have vanished." Something had vanished, all right—the parent himself!

Bryan dared a peek. The empty pants were gone. Spot cowered against the building with her T-shirt pulled over her face.

"Dad?" Bryan croaked. "Are you here?" He didn't want the empty pants to come back. But maybe Dad was inside. Perhaps he'd been splashed with invisible ink.

Spot peeped out from her T-shirt. "That way!" she squeaked, pointing.

Bryan scrambled to his feet, ready to run at the first glimpse of uninhabited pants. He couldn't freak out—he had to think! Even an invisible Dad would not walk away without saying a thing. So where could the real Dad be? Bryan's mind skipped back to the last time he'd seen his father: snoring away that morning in bed. But all he truly had seen were socks and a lump in the sheets. Dad might have been gone since last night!

"No, no . . . ," Bryan argued with the panic invading his head. The thing still tickling his throat must be affecting his eyes or his brain. Probably Dad was with Tripper. He had to find them both.

Tripper was closing the post office blinds when Bryan burst in.

"Where's my dad?" His legs shook. He'd sprinted the whole way. Spot stumbled into the doorway behind him.

Tripper raised her eyebrows. "I haven't seen him since yesterday, at your place."

"Neither have I! Just his clothes, and he wasn't inside them!"

"Legs!" Spot panted. "No head!"

"What are you two talking about?" Tripper asked, confused. Bryan was glad to have Spot backing him up.

"He's gone." He tried to explain, but his brain skipped. "Like your teabags. Without mice. He's been gone since last night!"

He doubled up, hacking. A small paper square fluttered onto the floor. He didn't have to look closer to know it was the tag from a teabag.

Without the slightest glance at the tag, Tripper trapped his shoulders with both hands. "You sound awful. Take a breath and calm down. And talk slower so I can understand. If it's like the mice, I know how you feel."

Bryan wriggled from her grasp. "I'm okay." His voice caught on a sob. He blamed the seed clogging his throat. "I just gotta find my dad."

"We'll find him," Tripper assured him. "When I left last night, he was heading after you. He knew you were upset. Didn't he catch up with you?"

Bryan shook his head and voiced his worst fear. "I'm afraid Mr. Keen got him."

Tripper frowned. "Got him? How?"

Bryan shot a look at Spot. Her mouth formed the V in *vampires!* Luckily, she stopped. There was too much to explain.

"Just come help me look for him," he pleaded with Tripper. "At Acme."

"No. You're staying right here." She reached for the phone. "We'll call the police. Then we'll—"

Grabbing Spot's arm, he dashed out. Tripper could call, but the nearest cops might be miles away. In the meantime, Bryan would search.

The pair ran down the street. As soon as Spot realized where they were headed, she skidded to a halt.

"Not Acme now!" she exclaimed. "It's gonna be dark soon."

"I've got to find my dad! Mr. Keen made him vanish. You've got to help!"

Spot shook her head so hard her pigtails whizzed past his face.

"Hey," Bryan complained, "I said I'd be your friend, no matter what. How about you? You're always running off mad or scared. What kind of friend is that?"

Spot grimaced and whined. Her hands yanked at her pigtails.

"This is a no-matter-what!" he insisted. "We'll be okay if we stick together. Come on." He marched toward the factory, resisting the urge to look back.

After a few steps, his heart flopped. She wasn't

coming. He was all on his own. Feeling like a lost pet, Bryan crushed his hands into fists, coughed up a hairball, and ran.

The Acme gate was locked. Pressing his nose on the guardhouse window didn't open it this time. Bryan couldn't spot Mr. Keen or any white robots. He shook the chain-link fence, glaring at the barbed wire on top.

Feet thumped behind him. He whirled. Spot ran up. She clutched Bryan's sleeve.

"No matter what," she gasped, trying to look in every direction at once.

Grateful, Bryan threw his arms around her. Then he turned and kicked the fence. "We've got to get in. I don't know where else to look!"

Spot examined the fence. She bent near its base and dug with her hands. Dirt flew between her legs. Impressed, Bryan joined her. Sometimes it paid to think like a dog.

Once they'd scooped a hole under the fence and shimmied through, they ran to the office. That was locked, too. No one answered their pounding. Frustrated, Bryan glared at the trucks parked nearby.

"Maybe my dad's tied up in one of those," he said, starting toward them.

"Don't think so," Spot said. She'd watched

through her binoculars almost all day, she told him. Acme robots and a few town employees had painted the trucks, inside and out. Other than paint, they were empty.

"Maybe they're not really trucks," she worried. "Maybe they're extra-large vampire coffins."

"Too drafty," Bryan declared. Spot's crazy fears made his own seem foolish, too. Feeling braver, he added, "My dad might be working on a broken-down truck. Let's look."

Spot followed so close they tripped over each other. The trucks were all silent and locked. Bryan led Spot around back. The dandelion field squeaked as new buds broke through the soil.

"Your dad isn't here, let's search somewhere else," Spot urged.

"Wait. I think we can sneak in through the Dumpster."

She gave him a funny look but followed him to it. He lifted the heavy lid. A twangy smell floated out from a jumble of Acme paint cans.

"Climb in and stand on those cans so you can hold the lid for me," he said.

Wary, Spot studied his face. "You'd better be right behind me!" she said. After his hearty nod, she boosted herself up. Once both her feet hit the trash, though, the cans slipped from beneath her.

"Yeow!" She disappeared into a clattering avalanche.

"Spot? You okay?" Propping the lid on his head, Bryan clambered up to see.

The bottom of the Dumpster was utterly black. Spot and the paint cans had vanished.

25

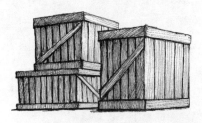

A CRACK IN THE PAINT

Bryan didn't think twice. He crawled over the edge and dropped in after Spot. The Dumpster lid clanged. All went black.

The metal beneath him tipped away. He slipped headfirst in the dark down a long, twisting slide. After a few panicked gasps, he spun himself so that his feet went down first, then dragged his palms and sneakers to slow his dizzying skid.

"Spot?" His voice echoed. "Dad?" The blackness thinned to gray. A flash of white appeared below and Bryan tumbled off the slide. To his surprise, it didn't hurt. He pawed through the cushy, white landing pad—dandelion seeds by the million.

The lid to a paint can bounced off his head. He looked up. A few glowing lights and the white ceiling stared back. There was no hint of the slide or the glass chute that Bryan remembered. There was no opening overhead big enough for the lid, let alone a boy or girl.

Spot sprawled nearby, surrounded by empty paint cans. She blew dandelion fluff from her bangs.

"Well, we're inside," she said. "At least it's not dark. You think we fell through the hole Mr. Keen's looking for?"

"No. He knows about the secret passage in the Dumpster."

"Can we go back out that way?"

"I don't see how," Bryan admitted. "Come on."

Together they swam to the edge of the fluff-filled bin and climbed out. Dandelion seeds spilled out with them, and more drifted around the nearby glassworks, scattered by the sudden disturbance.

"Dad? You in here?" called Bryan. The wafting fluff absorbed the sound like a sponge. It did not, however, hide the unbroken stretch of concrete walls around them. The red door was gone.

Gazing about, Spot groaned. "It looks like we're trapped."

"That can't be right." Bryan trotted the whole

way around, one hand sweeping the concrete for a crack or seam or invisible knob. After a long hunt, he met Spot in the middle.

"Told you," she said, without rancor.

"I'm sorry." Bryan exhaled hard, scattering white fluff. Sooner or later Mr. Keen would come for his dandelion seeds. But what was happening to Bryan's dad in the meantime? Or to him, for that matter? He clucked his tongue against the swollen back of his throat and murmured, "It's all my fault. Losing my dad, getting stuck in this place—everything."

"Don't say that. Maybe we can wish our way out," Spot suggested. She pinched one seed, held it in front of her lips, and squeezed her eyes tight. "I wish we were out of here—free as the birds." She blew.

Bryan wished she'd picked different words. He reached in with a crooked finger and drew a small finch from his mouth. Like a dove loosed from a top hat, it flapped into the air.

The idea of bird poop in his throat galvanized him. He hurried back to a corner where he'd kicked aside the Poof-Picker Pipe during his search for a door. He snatched it up. The hose was no longer attached. The vacuum at home hadn't worked, but that couldn't outsuck three tons of quicksand, could it? Before he could sneeze or cough up something else, Bryan tried bending both the pipebag's mouth-piece and its nozzle to his lips. Together, they wouldn't quite reach.

"Help me with this, will you?" he asked.

Spot had followed the bird toward the glittering glass machinery where Mr. Keen cooked invisible ink. When Bryan looked up she was poking and tweaking.

"Don't touch that!" he called. "I've got enough trouble already." He hurried over to stop her.

"If we turn it on," Spot argued, "maybe it'll make a noise, and someone will hear it and come let us out."

He realized she might be right. Acme certainly seemed to have a horn or alarm for everything else.

"Oh," she added, her face falling, "looks like it needs a battery."

Bryan snorted at the idea that something so large ran on so little power. Then he saw what she meant. Alongside a dot of green paint was a small nook the size of a nine-volt battery. Slim metal contacts and familiar + and − signs revealed its purpose. Spot pushed the green circle anyway. Nothing happened.

Gazing across the glass pipes and vials, Bryan spotted the Brussels sprouts he'd noticed before. He looked again at the battery compartment, remembered something he'd read, and stuffed his hand into his pocket.

"This is crazy," he said, "but I don't see how it could hurt."

Despite having spent a whole day and night in his pocket, the TaterNugget had remained firm. Both ends looked and felt exactly the same, but before he could doubt himself, Bryan slipped the pressed spud between the battery contacts.

With a chime and a tinkle, the glassworks trembled to life. Glass pistons pumped. A fan whirred, sending dandelion fluff shooting through clear tubes. Spot giggled, but the siren Bryan expected never came. The machine only plinked musically.

Spot lifted the nozzle Mr. Keen had shown Bryan. Waving it, she wondered, "Is this where the ink comes out?" Sticky white goo shot from its tip to splatter the floor.

"Oops. I guess not." She hastily replaced the nozzle.

"That's the leftovers, I think," Bryan said. "But listen—no alarm. We'd better turn it back off." He reached for the power supply only to yelp at the shock it gave him.

"Just let it run," Spot said, as he vainly pressed the green dot. "Someone might still come."

"Or it might overflow and drown us in invisible ink," Bryan argued. "Mr. Keen said so."

A look of horror came over Spot's face. She ran to bang on the walls.

"Help! Let us out!"

"Don't freak out yet," Bryan said. "It would take a lot of ink to fill this place up. Still . . ."

Ignoring him, she snatched a paint can and flung it against the wall with a clatter. The can wasn't quite empty. Black paint splattered, a dark slice against the white concrete.

"Hey. Look at this!" The paint sizzled.

Something whizzed past Bryan's ear. His finch flew smack into the dark blotch—and vanished.

Spot gasped. Bryan dashed over and stretched his fingers to the black swath.

"Careful!" she shouted. "Maybe it's acid!" Too late; Bryan's fingers passed into the wall and beyond.

"It made some kind of crack." He peered in. Eyes were useless in the inky darkness. He inched his hand farther into the slit. When he got as far as his shoulder, he waved his arm in the cool nothing on the other side of the wall.

"Something's going to grab you!" Spot fretted.

Bryan pulled his arm out. He put his lips to the crack and shouted, "Halloooo! Anybody out there? Dad, hey, Dad!" Not even an echo came back.

"Let's make it bigger," he said. "Maybe we can get out that way." He picked up Spot's can. It wasn't paint after all. The label read ACTIVE CHEMICAL FOR MAKING ENTRIES.

What they needed was an exit, he thought, but an entry might do. Using one sock like a sponge, he scooped up the black goo and wiped it on the wall. The gaping crack grew.

Bending over the label's instructions, Spot told him, "It says 'Apply Carefully to Minimize Errors.'"

In response, Bryan smoothed the edges down to the floor to make the dark area look less like a crack and more like a very large mouse hole.

"A cave?" Spot asked.

"A tunnel. To escape through." A rumbling began behind the wall.

"No way I'm going in there," she replied. "Something is growling."

Bryan poked his head into the tunnel. He still couldn't see anything.

Behind him, Spot grabbed his shirt. "Don't blame me if something bites off your head." Her voice sounded distant. The rumbling, however, grew louder. Recognizing it, Bryan backed out fast. There might not be much time.

26

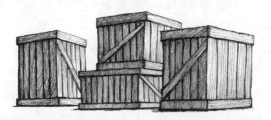

AN ABRUPT ENTRANCE

It's a train!" Standing on tiptoe, Bryan madly spread black to widen the arch.

The floor started to shake. The vibration rattled loose a few pipes in the inkworks. Soon a stream of fluff cascaded into the air.

With a deafening horn blast, a headlight shone from deep in the hole.

"Don't get run over!" Spot yanked Bryan away. The noise grew so loud they both clapped their hands to their ears. "Where the heck is it?" she yelled.

"Maybe it's stuck! The tunnel's not big enough!"

The can was almost wiped clean. He managed to swipe one last sockful.

"Boost me up there!" he said. "I'll make it taller."

"No! If it works, we'll get flattened!"

Just then the train's headlight went out. The chugging faded.

"Wait, come back!" Bryan shouted. "We need help!" But the two of them soon stood in silence again, a blizzard of white wishing seeds muffling everything.

"We could walk out, maybe," he suggested. "Follow the train tracks."

Giving him a crooked look, Spot edged toward the tunnel. She slid one foot into the darkness, then whisked it back right away.

"I can't," she moaned. "It's pitch-black. We'll be lost forever in there."

The idea of walking into the dark, perhaps headlong into a train, gave Bryan goose bumps, too. He sneezed. A flurry of goose down joined the fluff that fell around them and lay in drifts to their knees.

"Whatever you do, don't inhale any of these seeds," Bryan warned. He pulled the neck of his T-shirt up like a bandanna over his face. Between that and the puffiness in his throat, it grew even harder to breathe.

"We aren't going to drown, we're going to suffocate!" Spot wailed. "I don't want to die—dog or no dog!" She yanked off her collar and flung it to the floor. "I'm afraid I'll end up in mutt heaven! I want angels and chocolate, not chew bones and cats!"

Glad his T-shirt hid his lips, Bryan mashed them flat to crush a giggle. Then he pulled the shirt back down to talk. "We're not going to die," he reassured her. "I don't think you need to worry so much about turning into a dog, either. I'll give you pooch treats every day if it happens, but I bet it won't."

Doubt flickered over her face. Her eyes stole to her collar as if she felt unsafe without it.

"Leave it," he said. "If you disappear and some new dog shows up in town the same day, I'll make sure nobody thinks you're a stray. Until then, I'd rather have a best friend who was human."

A weak smile broke through her distress. "Really? You mean it?"

"Yes. But we have to get out of here fir—" Bryan coughed. A few kibbles bounced out.

Brightening, Spot prodded the dog food with her sneaker. "Hey, can you cough up something useful?" she asked. "Like a phone?" At his dubious expression, she added, "Try. Think about a cell phone. I'll look around for anything else we could use." She started wading through the waves of dandelion seeds.

Bryan turned back to the tunnel. Ignoring Spot's suggestion, he racked his brain for a way to escape. He still had one sockful of black goop; there had to be some way to use it. He didn't want to be discovered there by Mr. Keen or, worse, the police.

Bryan's shoulders drooped. He was closer to being the Crook than the Buster at this point. More important, he had to get out and find Dad. Who else could grill cheese sandwiches with a welding torch? Who else called him pal and tucked him into a bed on a hydraulic lift? Bryan would even share Dad with Tripper if he could just get him back.

Bryan gulped. Forget Acme's secrets. Right now he wished he'd never met Mr. Keen. If only the truck that had dropped off that crate had never appeared on Route 64.

An idea twisted to life within him. "Hmm. What if . . . ?"

He bent down, whisked aside the dandelion seeds near his feet, and swiped his gooey sock on the floor. Stepping back a few feet, he repeated it twice before the black was all gone. A rough dotted line now led from the tunnel smack into the center of the room.

"What's that?" Spot peered toward the line.

Honk! Honk! echoed out of the tunnel. The roar of an engine approached.

"A highway!" He tugged Spot out of the way. "The train couldn't fit, but maybe something else will!" The whine of speeding tires filled the room. A crack appeared in the top of the arch. Concrete dust sifted onto the floor.

Brakes squealed and—*kee-RASH!*—Bryan and Spot dove for a corner. Hunks of black tunnel and gray concrete flew. When the explosive burst settled, a battered tow truck stuck out of the wall where the tunnel had been. A shocked face peered from the cab.

"Tripper!" Bryan couldn't have been more relieved if his own mother had appeared. In fact, that unlikely event would have been shocking, not reassuring. Tripper, on the other hand, was as reliable as junk mail and twice as smart.

"What are you doing driving Dad's truck?" he exclaimed as she slid from the cab.

"Looking for you!" She clenched her eyes tight, then opened them wide. "The police said they were coming, but I got too worried to wait. I could hear you both yelling but couldn't see where. I thought of the mice. So I closed my eyes and followed my ears." She gazed around. "I guess I found you, but, boy—"

AAAOOOGA! split the air. The overhead lights flashed. Their intrusion had finally tripped an alarm.

Tripper yanked Spot and Bryan into the truck. When the engine rumbled to life, she shoved the gear stick into reverse, not bothering with the rearview mirror. The truck screeched back the way it had come.

Whirling, Bryan saw through the cab's rear window what Tripper had missed. His breath stopped. The parking lot should lie on the other side of the factory wall, but it didn't. What awaited instead was not part of this world.

27

HAVOC AT THE HOLE

S top!" Bryan cried.

With a horrid squelch, the truck's back end plowed into something squishy. A giant pink blob oozed out of the tunnel, enveloping the rear of the truck.

"Look!" Spot pointed. Mr. Keen was running toward them, his arms waving frantically.

"Get out!" the man yelled. "Get out of that truck!"

They scrambled to obey. The blob surged to swallow the truck, pulsing like an enormous pink jellyfish. When the alarm stopped abruptly, Bryan heard muted crunching instead.

"That was close," said Mr. Keen. He exhaled hard through pursed lips.

"Do you see *that*?" Bryan asked Tripper.

"More than I want to!" She cringed, pulling Bryan and Spot closer.

"A mouthful of fillings couldn't insulate her eyeballs at this range," Mr. Keen told Bryan. "That much muffling would take braces, at least."

"What is it, for heaven's sake?" Tripper demanded.

"It looks like bubble gum," said Mr. Keen. "Bubble-gum blobs have swallowed whole towns. Good thing this one's got something big to chew on for a moment."

He turned to clap Bryan on the back. "You found the hole! Or to be more precise, it found you."

"It did?" Bryan gulped. He should be excited, even proud, but watching the pink lump chew on the truck, he mostly felt stunned.

"I knew it would, sooner or later. The I-zone is tricky, and holes can slink around just out of sight, leaking worse all the time before they finally burst through. Your curiosity worked like a magnet, drawing it out—as planned, I might add, if I do say so myself. Curiosity, Imagination, Trouble: stir up one and you'll soon find the others. I just had to hope we could tease out the hole before too much Trouble leaked through."

"Oh, you've got trouble, all right," Tripper grumbled. "Just wait till the authorities hear about this."

A smile tugged at Mr. Keen's lips. "What makes you think they don't know?"

Tripper stammered.

"Imaginative stuff is supposed to leak into the world," he continued. "Just not quite so much. Now that Bryan and Spot have uncovered it, we can simply plug up the rip between the dimensions. Then the I-zone will work right again."

"The what-zone?" Tripper stared from the blob to the glassworks, still spewing white fuzz.

"The I-zone. The layer of Imagination surrounding the earth."

"I thought imagination was something in your head," Spot said.

"Is gravity in your head?" countered Mr. Keen. "Electricity? Radio waves? Your head just helps you know how to use them. Same with I-juice. It can be dangerous, though. That's why Acme is here. We can't let raw inspiration leak completely unchecked. When it does . . ."

"Blobs," Bryan guessed.

"Vampires," shivered Spot.

The Acme boss nodded. "Exploding cupcakes,

flying monkeys . . . Trouble. Large leaks cause panic. That's why we find them and fix them." He looked sideways at Bryan and Spot. "And that's why I hired you—little leak magnets. I hope you don't mind."

"I guess not," Bryan said. "But what did you do with my dad?"

Mr. Keen shuffled his feet. "You noticed. He hasn't reappeared yet?"

"Last time I saw him he was invisible!" Bryan shouted.

Spot added, "Except for his pants."

"What did you do to him?" Tripper grabbed Mr. Keen's arm.

"Nothing," he protested. "Nothing much, anyway. I just turned back his clock." He spun his finger near his head. The motion reminded Bryan of the clock hands that twirled on the Acme office ceiling. Twitching an eyebrow at him, Mr. Keen added, "To a time before he told you to quit. He should have caught up by now, though." He checked his watch. "Yes, indeed. It's practically bedtime. So I would expect him to be somewhere around six o'clock."

The tall man surveyed the room. "Let's see. If this is our noon"—he pointed straight toward the blob, then turned to the right—"then this would be three o'clock, and that would be . . . yes! There he is. Just after six."

Bryan spun. A shadow wavered inside the mountains of dandelion fluff.

"Dad!" Plowing through a curtain of white, Bryan slammed into a familiar plaid shirt that felt wonderfully stuffed. Overjoyed, he grabbed on and didn't let go.

"Brn!" Dad hugged him. "Thansfrwameup!"

Bryan stared up at the smiling face. Dad's speech sounded like a recording on fast forward.

"He's still a few hours behind," explained Mr. Keen. "Still catching up."

"Youldn'tblevedreamIshaving. I—" Dad looked around. He waved one hand so fast through the dandelion seeds that his fingers blurred. "Maybbyould," he added. "Yourinttoo."

"It's not a dream, Dad." Bryan pulled his father toward the others.

"Are you all right?" Tripper asked. Dad nodded double-time, his eyes glued on the blob. Bryan figured they could wait to mention the truck.

"Imittlecofusedtho," Dad managed. "Wharwe? Wyrutaknsoslo? Whasgonon?"

"No time to explain all over again," announced

Mr. Keen. "Now that our leaky hole can be seen, it must be plugged u—"

A monstrous groan emerged from the bubble-gum blob. Two pink, sticky lips split apart. With a huge belch, the blob spit a truck tire at them.

Tripper screamed. In a flash, Dad yanked them all to the floor. The tire flew over their heads before bouncing across the room. The thuds ended in a shimmering crash and a long rain of tinkles, plinks, jingles, and chimes.

Mr. Keen staggered back to his feet. "The . . . it . . . no!"

The tire rested in a carpet of shards. Not a single flask or tube of the glass inkworks remained.

"Uh-oh," Bryan said. "No more invisible ink."

"Hu . . . hu . . . huuuuu," rumbled the blob. Bryan was sure it was laughing.

Mr. Keen clapped his hands to his head and crumpled like a rag doll. "The ink's not the half of it. What will we do?" He gazed dully at Bryan's dad. "Your tire destroyed our only hope of plugging the hole."

"Snotmyfault," Dad protested.

"It was the blob!" Bryan said.

"The blame hardly matters!" Mr. Keen ranted. "That Poof Press was vital for distilling all this fluff into anything useful! Once the ink is pressed out, what's left is Acme's hole-patching compound—far more valuable than the ink!"

Remembering the nozzle and the white stickum that had splattered onto the floor, Bryan and Spot swapped a guilty glance.

"No Poof Press—no patch!" Mr. Keen wailed. "And with no patch . . ." He gestured.

The blob had drawn back from the edge of the hole. Picking through the rubble around it were visions and nightmares of all sorts. First Bryan saw a giant green caterpillar and what looked like a beach ball with teeth. A strolling fairy-tale princess, raising a mirror in front of her face, promptly vanished. Springs slithered and boinged into the room like sinister Slinkies. Worse, Bryan spotted red eyes gleaming in the darkness behind the pink blob. He and Spot both clasped their hands to their necks.

The approaching frights spurred the adults into action. Tripper swept Bryan and Spot into her arms while Bryan's dad clutched Mr. Keen by the lapels. Bryan felt a surge of fear for both men.

"Getusoutofear!" Dad hollered.

Mr. Keen kept his eyes fixed on the hole. "The best dental work in the world won't drown out I-zone leaking like that!" he shouted. "The dullest nincompoops will notice. South Wiggot might become worse than—" He clacked his teeth together and dragged his gaze back to the others. He wiped his long fingers down his face. "Ahem. I'm forgetting my duties. Let's just say that in six centuries of covert operations, the I.I.I.I. has never faced a disaster like this."

"Ai-yi-yi-yi-yi?" Tripper repeated, her voice shrill.

"There has to be some way to fix it," Bryan said. He slipped loose from Tripper but kept close track of those red eyes in the dark. Even Dad might be no match for those.

"We have to try, don't we? Or crazy ideas will run rampant." Mr. Keen cast a gloomy look at the mounds of dandelion fluff on the floor. "The raw material is undamaged, at least. What a mess."

"Can we push it in there by hand?" Bryan shoved fluff toward the hole.

Spot watched doubtfully. "We're gonna stop vampires with dandelion seeds?"

"Not just seeds." Mr. Keen wagged his head. "Wishes. Powerful stuff, especially when it hits raw inspiration. But without the Poof Press"—he waved toward the shattered glass—"I don't know how we can squish the wishes enough."

Indeed, the harder Bryan scooped, the faster the fluff drifted away. The adults watched dubiously.

Spot squealed. While all eyes had been following Bryan's attempt, an ape wearing a baseball cap had burst from the hole. Now it snatched Spot from Tripper and tucked her under its arm like a football.

"Spot!" Bryan yelled.

Tripper threw a chunk of concrete. She only knocked the ape's cap off.

Bryan's dad hoisted a bigger hunk and ran toward the beast. The ape screamed even louder than Spot. It dashed back into the hole, hauling the girl with it.

"Never mind! We can get her back later!" Mr. Keen shouted. "We've got to plug that leak before it

gets any worse or South Wiggot is doomed! Perhaps the whole state!"

"What about this?" Bryan yanked the Poof-Picker Pipe from the rubble. He raised the mouthpiece to his lips and blew like he'd never blown before.

"Wait!"

Mr. Keen's warning proved useless. The massive sucking power was already working. Fluff jiggled. Fluff wobbled. Then the whole roomful of fluff rolled and roared in a huge wave toward Bryan. Excited, he blew even harder.

That's when he remembered. There was no hose attached to the pipebag as there had been outside. Without it, he didn't know where the poof would end up.

The last thing Bryan saw was an avalanche of fluff.

28

PLUGGED UP

Bryan sat up, his head cottony and confused. White wisps stuck to his eyelashes. He'd been knocked flat by the tidal wave of dandelion seeds, and now his collar, his cuffs, and even his undies were crammed so full of fluff that he felt like an overstuffed sofa. That wasn't the worst, though. The familiar tickle in his throat matched fuzzy feelings in his ears and nose and belly because his insides were stuffed as full as his clothes. Without the hose attached, the Poof-Picker Pipe must have backed up, sucking the whole roomful of seeds into him.

"Are you okay?" Dad, Tripper, and Mr. Keen bent over him, concern sharp on their faces.

His cheeks puffed out like basketballs, Bryan tried to answer "I think so." Only a muffled garble came out, so he nodded instead. When he exhaled, two white jets streamed from his nose like steam from an old-fashioned train. That must have made space for the air going in.

"That can't be good for your brain," Tripper said. "Spit it out!"

"I imagine it's quite stuck in such a small space," Mr. Keen said. "There must be a kazillion poofs in that boy."

Dad didn't waste time talking. He yanked fluff from between Bryan's teeth. Even at his abnormal speed, he'd be plucking for days.

Then that darn old tickle in Bryan's throat began to get stronger. His eyelids jiggled, and he waved his hands helplessly. He knew what that feeling meant. The one seed festering in his throat all afternoon was preparing again to launch something strange. This time the passage was blocked.

"NNNgrrbleflll!" Bryan yelled. Nose itching, teeth tingling, he jumped to his feet. Spotting the Poof-Picker Pipe, he pointed and stomped. Mr. Keen lifted the pipebag but shook his head sadly. The bag must have exploded when all those seeds whisked through at once. Tatters were all that remained.

Bryan's eyes rolled. He wasn't sure how anyone could help him, but his nose tickled all the way to his brain. With an enormous sneeze pending, the next thing to explode might be his head!

"Dosomthng!" Dad grabbed Mr. Keen. Tripper slapped Bryan's shoulders, trying to knock wish seeds out. His eyes started to water, and he rubbed his nose as hard as he could. Maybe he could make the gathering sneeze go away.

Mr. Keen's eyes lit up. "Superb idea! Let me help!" He whipped a peacock feather out of one sleeve and twitched the green tip beneath Bryan's nose.

That maddening tickle finished it. Bryan closed his eyes. He didn't expect to survive. The last few moments passed behind his dark eyelids: the tow truck, the blob, the ape carting off Spot. If the others weren't simply consumed by the blob, he hoped they'd at least rescue Spot.

"Aaaahhh . . . aaaaahhhhhh . . ."

A last-minute idea flashed into Bryan's mind. His eyes flew open. *Dandelion seeds, think only of dandelion seeds,* he told himself. *Fluffy, floaty, tickly, and sticky with spit*. He ran toward the gaping hole in the wall, dodging a fleet of pint-sized UFOs. The pink blob still chomped away in the shadows. Sensing his approach, it surged forward.

"Chhhooooooo!" Bryan flew off his feet one way. The fluff crammed inside him spewed out the other. He landed hard on his back pockets, his eyes on the wish wad. It bounced off the bubble gum and splattered back to cover the hole.

Buzzing, the UFOs tried to dart back inside. They ricocheted off the thick patch. Behind it, the blob shoved. Bryan's makeshift plaster bulged—but held fast.

"You're a genius!" cried Mr. Keen. He ran to help Bryan to his feet. Dad followed quickly to be sure he was safe.

"Better yet, I'm alive," Bryan said. It was wonderful to make words again. His mouth had never felt so parched, and his stretched cheeks drooped, but nothing tickled inside anymore. He wiggled his tongue, just for fun. His dad pulled him into a hug.

Mr. Keen poked at the patch on the wall. "Your extraordinary sneeze appears to have worked as well as our usual methods—perhaps better! Admirably done."

He folded in a deep bow. Pride swirled through

Bryan. When his father stepped back and stuck out a huge hand, Bryan accepted the handshake with a tingle.

His joy lasted less than a second.

"What about Spot?" Tripper asked. She had found the cast-off collar and was twisting it between her hands.

Mr. Keen jerked upright. The smile fell from his face. He stared at the patched wall, tapping his chin. "We can't leave her trapped in the I-zone, can we? Hmm." He turned on his heel and marched directly to a red door in the wall. "Follow me."

"Hey!" Bryan said. "That door wasn't there a few minutes ago!"

"Of course not." Mr. Keen cast him a pointed glance. "Only *trespassers* were here a few minutes ago. Now you've shown yourself to be much more important."

Rushing to follow his boss through the doorway, Bryan was no longer surprised when they didn't come out in the lobby but rather in a storeroom stacked with large crates. The Acme logo had been stenciled on each, like the crate Mr. Keen had arrived in.

"What's in all these?" Tripper wanted to know.

Mr. Keen planted his hands on his hips to survey the room. "Sometimes we don't know until we open the lid. Sometimes we're sorry we did!" He turned to Bryan. "See one that might appeal to Spot?"

"Thrallalike," protested Dad.

"No. Don't listen to that." Mr. Keen bent near Bryan's ear, his voice low. "They are no more alike than you and anyone else in South Wiggot. Do I make myself clear?"

Bryan gave Mr. Keen an uncertain look. Before he could open his mouth, the old spirals appeared in those olive green eyes. This close there could be no mistake.

"Try tapping into the I-zone a bit," Mr. Keen added. "You've proven an expert at that." One eye winked. The spirals vanished.

With that wink, Bryan understood. It was all in how he saw things. Most things he saw with a bit of a twist. He alone controlled that, and he knew Spot best.

He studied the crates. At first the wood shapes all looked the same, as Dad had suggested. But as he kept gazing, he could see a bit more. Many were rectangles, while others were square. Some hinted at teepees or crescents or Zs. A few bulged or wobbled as Bryan looked on.

Then he spied a small crate alone in one corner. Its

top rose to a peak like a lopsided doghouse. Bryan pointed. "There."

Sure enough, when Mr. Keen rapped on that crate, something inside banged back. Dad helped pry off the lid. Spot popped out, bubble gum tangling her hair. A banana peel was slung over one shoulder.

"It was smelly and sticky and dark!" She panted in relief as the adults helped her climb out. "I was sure I was stuck in a vampire coffin!"

"You're safe now," Mr. Keen said. "Thank Bryan for that."

Spot threw her arms around Bryan. She smelled like bananas, but the hug still made him feel welcome and warm.

"No matter what," he mumbled.

"Best friends," she replied.

"Are you sure you're all right, Spot?" Tripper plucked off the banana peel, fussed with Spot's gooey hair, and offered her back the lost dog collar.

Spot eyed the metal-studded strap a long moment, then tossed it over her shoulder into the crate. "Spot decided to stay in the I-zone," she declared with a smile. "I'm Rebecca."

"A dunk in the I-zone does sometimes spark a new start," their boss noted.

"But how'd she get into the crate?" Tripper wondered.

"From thape?" added Dad, his speed getting closer to everyone else's.

"The I-zone doesn't flow in straight lines," Mr. Keen told them. "It's more . . . well . . . curly and sideways. It's hard to explain." He glanced at Bryan. "Except to people who know how—and aren't afraid—to use it."

"I didn't plug it up too much, did I?" Bryan asked.

The Acme chief snorted. "Impossible. The I-zone leaks like a fishnet. We only bother with the big holes. That's where Trouble gets through."

"I still think it must be toxic waste," Tripper grumbled.

"No." Mr. Keen shrugged. "But this Trouble is over. Believe what you want."

"Iblieve istime togohome," Dad said. "Ivad enough trouble froneday."

"Quite right," replied Mr. Keen. "Come along. You've seen too much as it is."

29

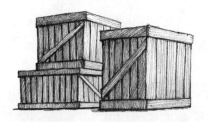

THE I.I.I.I.I.

When Bryan finally crawled into bed that night, he expected nightmares about exploding heads. Instead, he dreamed of floating through blue skies with brilliant white wish seeds. Life was fine.

The morning sun brought a shock, though. Acme was gone. The building, the guardhouse, the Dumpster, the fence—the whole kaboodle had vanished. Nothing remained but a field of weeds. South Wiggot townsfolk gossiped about it for weeks. Some said those strange Acme employees blew the building to pieces and hauled off the chunks in the trucks. Others swore they saw the whole thing blast into space.

Spot and Bryan knew better. "It's like the Bermuda Triangle," Spot whispered. "Sometimes things vanish."

"The South Wiggot Triangle, you could say," Bryan replied. "Mr. Keen just knows how to get around through the I-zone."

After a few days without any odd vision or sound, he could almost believe that none of it had happened. His stretched cheeks bounced back right away. That meant his only real evidence, besides his new bank account, lay in a few shreds of confetti and two pieces of seven.

There was the tow truck, of course. They never saw it again. At first Dad grumbled over the loss.

"You never towed with it anyhow," Tripper pointed out. "Maybe we can use the insurance money as a down payment on a house." Bryan stopped listening then. The evening at Acme had made them more of a team, since they couldn't talk about it with anyone else. Bryan got more attention than Oscar now, too. Nobody said "Oh, it's just you" when he walked into a room. Although Tripper was teasing when she called him the savior of South Wiggot, it always made him grin, and he knew he could count on her for more than pancakes and laughs. But the idea of living with her was still new enough to make him nervous.

For a week or so after the factory vanished, he also felt sad. Mr. Keen had left without even saying good-bye.

Then one morning, Bryan decided to eat cereal for breakfast. He was pouring his Crispy Ts when a folded slip of paper tumbled into the bowl. Assuming it was only a coupon, he tossed it aside.

Halfway through a crunchy mouthful, he noticed the warning on the slip: "Do not dampen with milk. Not tasty at all. If misdirected, please forward to the South Wiggot Zoom-Juice establishment."

Bryan dropped his spoon. His hands shook with excitement as he unfolded the slip. Only one person could have sent a note with a warning like that.

"Apologies," it said. "Had to leave fast. Leaks spring all the time. We can hardly keep up.

"I've put in a request," it went on. "I think you'd make a strong undercover agent for the I.I.I.I.I. You'll keep this top secret, of course. No one would believe you anyhow. We'll be in touch. Keen."

Bryan never finished his breakfast. He raced to Spot's house to find her sitting on her porch, an identical note in her hands.

"What's the I.I.I.I.I.?" Bryan asked. He remembered seeing I^5 in the contract, but that didn't help. "He never said what the letters stand for."

Spot didn't know either. Whenever her brother wasn't around, she and Bryan hijacked his computer to search the Internet. They couldn't find anything with so many *I*s. If they stumbled on a promising Web site or link, the next click always resulted in "File Not Found" or, worse, "No permission to access this site." Eventually they gave up.

Bryan went back to selling LemonMoo by the side of the road. Spot often kept him company there. She'd been forced to cut most of her hair to get the bubble gum out, but the new look helped people remember to call her Rebecca. To Bryan, however, she'd always be Spot.

With her help, his business was better than ever. They found that if they flipped his gold coins as a car approached, the driver nearly always stopped to buy a drink. Bryan might never be a LemonMoo Legend, but by the time school started, he'd have enough cash to buy the computer he wanted.

It wouldn't be long before the school bus started its rounds again, either. Bryan began to think Mr. Keen had forgotten about them. Or perhaps he'd been swallowed by a bubble-gum blob or another I-zone leak that was even worse. Bryan wished he could call his old boss on the phone.

One night in bed, the lumpy pillowcase files under his head gave him an idea.

The next morning, he dug a balloon and a faded old grocery receipt from the junk drawer. He addressed one side of the receipt: "To Mr. Keen, Acme Inc. Private!" On the other he wrote, "Hi. We miss you and hope you're okay. What's the I^5? I promise I'll never tell anyone but Spot."

He reread his note to make sure it wouldn't give away any secrets if it fell into the wrong hands. Then he signed it, rolled it up, and stuffed it through the neck of the balloon. Blown up and knotted, the round rubber envelope concealed his message inside. He and Spot climbed the tree that grew near the factory site. They released the balloon to the wind. Without helium, it didn't soar, but the breeze whisked it over the fields.

Bryan trudged home. He decided he didn't like I-mail, or whatever the I^5 would call it. It would be torture to get through every day wondering if Mr. Keen had received his message at all.

When he went to mix his next batch of Lemon-Moo, though, the milk carton felt awfully light. He tipped it carefully over his pitcher. A white business card tumbled out.

At first Bryan thought it was blank. Then he guessed that the message must be printed with invisible ink. Unfortunately, he had no idea how to make it visible to read it. He tried sprinkling it with lemon juice and rubbing it with a bit of potato. He held it in front of a candle, a magnet, a clock, and a mirror. He looked at it under a black light and through broken glass. No use. Bryan guessed it might be a test. If so, he was failing.

Spot helped solve the problem. "What about dandelion light?" she suggested. "You know, you hold a dandelion under your chin and it glows."

"Yeah, so?" It was some girl thing, Bryan thought. If your chin glowed, it meant you had a boyfriend or something goofy like that.

Spot plucked a fat golden bloom from the roadside. She poked it at Bryan. "Try it on your card. Maybe it'll light up the invisible ink."

Bryan pulled the blank card from his pocket. He held it over the flower. He and Spot banged their heads as they both bent to look underneath.

There, in the bloom's slight yellow glow, small golden letters appeared on the card. Spot held it up while Bryan kneeled below, craned his neck, and read aloud.

"'International Institute for the Investigation of

Imaginative Incidents'—that's five *I*s!" he crowed. "Beneath, it says, 'Ideas, Inventions, Illusions, and Invisible Ink also for sale. Inquire at Acme Inc. for information.' That's all. Turn it over."

The back of the card held more golden words. Bryan squinted. With his heart beating hard, he made out the tiny print: "Message intercepted. Welcome to the Special Agent ranks of the I.I.I.I.I. Agent Keen informed us of your influence in the South Wiggot incident. Appreciate your initiative and intelligent involvement in that important intervention. No immediate insight about impending instances near you. Inform us of anything interesting. Identify your-selves only as Zero and Woof in the future. Stay incognito and stand by for assignment. We know where to find you. I^5."

"Let me see!" shouted Spot. While she lifted the dandelion and the card over her head, Bryan smirked at the heat waves on the highway. His skin tingled with the pleasure of such a great secret. He didn't know how long it would be until they got an assign-ment, but he could wait. Maybe they'd see Mr. Keen again then. Perhaps they'd help patch another hole in the I-zone. The next time he saw a flat rubber dog or pants walking around by themselves, he'd know what to do.

In the meantime, Bryan thought, Special Agent Zero sounded good. Zero was only one letter off from Hero, after all, and a *Z* was just a sideways *H* with a twist. Plus, a Crookbuster of the Week got to be on TV, but seven days later was no one again. A Special Agent was special for life. Duty might call anytime.

Bryan grinned. He hoped he would get to answer that call with a ride in a big wooden crate.